Agatha Christie (1890-1976) is known throughout the world as the Queen of Crime. Her books have sold over a billion copies in English with another billion in over 100 foreign languages. She is the most widely published and translated author of all time and in any language; only the Bible and Shakespeare have sold more copies. She is the author of 80 crime novels and short story collections, 19 plays, and six other novels. *The Mousetrap*, her most famous play, was first staged in 1952 in London and is still performed there – it is the longest-running play in history.

Agatha Christie's first novel was published in 1920. It featured Hercule Poirot, the Belgian detective who has become the most popular detective in crime fiction since Sherlock Holmes. Collins has published Agatha Christie since 1926.

This series has been especially created for readers worldwide whose first language is not English. Each story has been shortened, and the vocabulary and grammar simplified to make it accessible to readers with a good intermediate knowledge of the language.

The following features are included after the story:

A **List of characters** to help the reader identify who is who, and how they are connected to each other. **Cultural notes** to explain historical and other references. A **Glossary** of words that some readers may not be familiar with are explained. There is also a **Reco**

Agatha Christie

Hickory Dickory Dock

Collins

Collins

HarperCollins Publishers
77-85 Fulham Palace Road
London W6 8JB

www.collinselt.com

Collins ® is a registered trademark of HarperCollins Publishers Limited.

This *Collins English Readers* edition published 2012

Reprint 10 9 8 7 6 5 4 3 2 1 0

First published in Great Britain by Collins 1955

ISBN: 978-0-00-745171-5

A catalogue record for this book is available from the British Library.

Cover by crushed.co.uk © HarperCollins/Agatha Christie Ltd 2008

Typeset by Aptara in India.

Printed and bound in Great Britain by Clays Ltd, St Ives plc.

Contents

Chapter 1

Hercule Poirot frowned.

'Miss Lemon,' he said.

'Yes, Monsieur Poirot?'

'There are three mistakes in this letter.'

He sounded shocked. Miss Lemon, a proud and professional woman, never made mistakes. She was never ill, never tired, never upset, never inaccurate. Order and method had been Hercule Poirot's favourite words for many years. With George, his perfect manservant, and Miss Lemon, his perfect secretary, order and method shaped his life.

And yet, this morning, Miss Lemon had made three mistakes in typing a very simple letter. The world had stopped turning.

Hercule Poirot held out the offending document. He was not annoyed, he was just confused. This was something that just could not happen – but it had!

Miss Lemon took the letter. 'Oh, dear, I can't think how I did that – well, perhaps I can. It's because of my sister.'

'Your sister?' Another shock. Poirot had never known that Miss Lemon had a sister.

Miss Lemon nodded. 'Yes, most of her life she has lived in Singapore. Her husband was in the rubber business there, but he died four years ago. There were no children, so when she came back to England I found a very nice little flat for her but – ' Miss Lemon paused. 'Well, she was lonely and she told me that she was thinking about taking a job.'

'Job?'

'Looking after a hostel for students. It is owned by a woman who is partly Greek and she wanted someone to manage it for her. It's a big old house and my sister was going to have a very nice flat – '

Miss Lemon stopped and Poirot made an encouraging noise for her to continue.

'I wasn't sure about it, but my sister likes to be busy and she's always been good with young people.'

'So your sister took the job?' Poirot asked.

'Yes, she moved into 26 Hickory Road about six months ago and she liked her work there.'

Hercule Poirot listened. So far, the story of Miss Lemon's sister had been disappointingly ordinary.

'But for some time now she's been very worried.'

'Why?'

'Well, Monsieur Poirot, she doesn't like the things that are going on there.'

'There are students there of both sexes?' Poirot inquired delicately.

'Oh no, I don't mean *that*! One always expects difficulties of *that* kind! No, but things have been disappearing.'

'Disappearing?'

'Yes. And such odd things . . . And all in rather a strange way.'

'When you say things have been disappearing, you mean things have been stolen?'

'Yes.'

'Have the police been called in?'

'No. My sister is fond of these young people – well, of some of them – and she would prefer to straighten things out by herself.'

'Yes,' said Poirot. 'I can understand that. But that does not explain, if I may say so, your own anxiety.'

'I cannot help feeling that something is going on which I do not understand. No ordinary explanation seems to fit with the facts.'

Poirot nodded. 'Not an ordinary thief? A kleptomaniac, perhaps?'

'I do not think so. I read about the subject, in the *Encyclopaedia Britannica*. But I was not persuaded.'

Hercule Poirot was silent for a minute and a half. Did he wish to involve himself in the troubles of Miss Lemon's sister? But it was very inconvenient to have Miss Lemon making mistakes in his letters. He told himself that *if* he were to involve himself, that would be the reason. He did not admit to himself that he had been rather bored lately.

'Supposing, Miss Lemon, you were to invite your sister here for afternoon tea? I might be able to be of some small help to her.'

'That's very kind of you, Monsieur Poirot.'

'Then shall we say tomorrow?'

Chapter 2

Miss Lemon's sister, Mrs Hubbard, looked very like her. She was a little fatter, her hair was more stylish, and she was gentler in manner, but her eyes were the same sharp eyes that shone through Miss Lemon's glasses.

'This is very kind of you, Monsieur Poirot,' she said. '*Very* kind. And such a wonderful tea, too.'

'First, we enjoy our tea – afterwards we talk business.' Poirot smiled at her and stroked his moustache. 'Can you explain to me exactly what worries you?'

'Yes, I can. It would be natural for money to be taken. And jewellery - that's natural too – well, I don't really mean natural – but it would make sense. So I'll just read you a list of the things that have been taken.' Mrs Hubbard opened her bag and took out a small notebook.

Evening shoe (one of a new pair)
Bracelet (cheap)
Diamond ring (found in a plate of soup)
Powder compact
Lipstick
Stethoscope
Old grey trousers
Electric light bulbs
Box of chocolates
Silk scarf (cut to pieces)
Rucksack (cut to pieces)
Boracic powder
Bath salts
Cookery book

Hercule Poirot took a long, deep breath. 'Very – very interesting. I congratulate you, Mrs Hubbard.'

She looked surprised. 'But why, Monsieur Poirot?'

'I congratulate you on having such an unusual and beautiful problem.'

'Well, perhaps it makes sense to you, Monsieur Poirot, but – '

'It does not make sense at all. Why was such a strange collection of things stolen? Is there any system there? The first thing to do is to study the list of objects very carefully.'

There was a silence while Poirot did this. When he finally spoke, Mrs Hubbard jumped.

'The first thing that I notice is this,' said Poirot. 'Most of the things were of small value, except for two – a stethoscope and a ring. Forget the stethoscope for a moment, I would like to concentrate on the ring. You say a diamond ring?'

'Yes, it had been Miss Lane's mother's engagement ring. She was most upset when it was missing, and we were all relieved when it reappeared the same evening in Miss Hobhouse's plate of soup. Just an unpleasant joke, we thought.'

'And so it may have been. But I myself think for someone to steal the ring and then return, it *is* important. If a lipstick, or a powder compact or a book are missing, you do not call in the police. But a diamond ring is different. It is very likely that the police *will* be called in. So the ring is returned.'

'But why take it if you're going to return it?' said Miss Lemon.

'That is a good question,' said Poirot. 'But for the moment we will forget questions. I am concentrating now on the objects. Who is this Miss Lane from whom the ring was stolen?'

'Patricia Lane? She's a very nice girl who's studying Histor

'Rich?'

'She's got a little money, but she doesn't have many new cl

‘What is she like?’

‘Well, she’s neither dark nor fair and rather quiet. A serious type of girl.’

‘And the ring was found in Miss Hobhouse’s plate of soup. Who is Miss Hobhouse?’

‘Valerie Hobhouse? She’s a clever girl with dark hair and rather a sharp manner. She works in a beauty salon, Sabrina Fair.’

‘Are these two girls friendly?’

Mrs Hubbard thought. ‘I think so – Patricia gets on well with everybody really. Valerie has her enemies, but she’s got her admirers too, if you know what I mean.’

‘I think I know,’ said Poirot. He looked at the list again. ‘What is so interesting is the different groups of things. There are the cheap articles and then we have the stethoscope, which someone might want to sell. Who did it belong to?’

‘Mr Bateson – he’s a big, friendly young man.’

‘A medical student?’

‘Yes.’

‘Was he very angry?’

‘Yes, Monsieur Poirot.’

‘And who did the grey trousers belong to?’

‘Mr McNabb. They were very old, but Mr McNabb is fond of his old clothes and he never throws anything away.’

‘So we have come to the things that seem not worth stealing – old trousers, light bulbs, boracic powder, bath salts – a cookery book. The boracic was probably taken by mistake; the cookery book may have been borrowed and not returned. Then there is the evening shoe, one of a new pair? Who do they belong to?’

‘Sally Finch. She’s an American girl studying Science over ... on a scholarship. She was going to a party in evening dress and the shoes were really important because they were her only evening shoes.'

'It was inconvenient – and annoying for her – yes. Yes, perhaps there is something there . . .' He was silent for a moment. 'And there are two more articles – a rucksack and a silk scarf, both cut to pieces. Here we have something that may be cruel. Who did the rucksack belong to?'

'Nearly all the students have rucksacks and many of them are the same – bought at the same place. But this one belonged to Leonard Bateson.'

'And the silk scarf. To whom did that belong?'

'To Valerie Hobhouse.'

'Miss Hobhouse . . . I see.'

Poirot closed his eyes. Pieces of silk scarf and rucksack, cookery books, lipsticks, names and pictures of students spun round in space. But Poirot knew that somewhere there must be a pattern . . . He opened his eyes. 'This is a matter that needs some consideration. But we might start with practical things. The evening shoe – yes, we might start with that. Miss Lemon, Mrs Hubbard will obtain for you, perhaps, the remaining shoe. Go with it to Baker Street Station, to the lost property department. You will say you left a shoe on a bus. How many buses pass near Hickory Road?'

'Two only, Monsieur Poirot.'

'Good.'

'But why do you think – ' began Mrs Hubbard.

Poirot interrupted her. 'Let us see first what results we get. Then you and I must talk again. You will tell me then those things which are necessary for me to know.'

'I really think I've told you everything I can.'

'No, no. Here we have young people all living together different characters, different sexes. A loves B, but B loves and D and E hate each other because of A perhaps. It is all *that* I need to know.'

'I'm sure,' said Mrs Hubbard uncomfortably, 'I don't know anything about *that* sort of thing.'

'But you are interested in people. You will tell me – yes, you will tell me! Because you are worried – not about what has been happening – you could go to the police about that – '

'The owner, Mrs Nicoletis, would not like to have the police called in, I can tell you that.'

Poirot paid no attention to this and continued, 'No, you are worried about *someone* – someone who you think may have been involved in this. Someone, therefore, that you like.'

'Really, Monsieur Poirot!'

'Yes, really. And I think you are right to be worried. For that silk scarf cut to pieces, it is not nice. And the rucksack, that also is not nice. The rest it seems like childishness – and yet – I am not sure. I am not sure at all!'

Chapter 3

Hurrying up the steps, Mrs Hubbard put her key into the door of 26 Hickory Road. Just as it opened, a big young man with red hair ran up behind her.

'Hallo, Ma, have you been out having fun?'

'I've been out to tea, Mr Bateson.'

'I cut up a beautiful dead body today,' said Len. 'That was fun!'

'A beautiful dead body! Really, you are awful.'

Len Bateson laughed.

A thin young man with untidy hair came out of a room on the right, and said sharply, 'Oh, it's only *you.* I thought because of the noise it must be at least a *group* of big men.'

'I hope it doesn't harm your nerves,' replied Bateson.

'Not more than usual,' said Nigel Chapman, and went back into his room.

'Our delicate flower,' said Len.

'Now don't you two quarrel,' said Mrs Hubbard. 'I like everyone to be friendly.'

The big young man smiled down at her. 'I don't mind Nigel, Ma.'

'Oh, Mrs Hubbard, Mrs Nicoletis is in her room and said she would like to see you as soon as you got back.' A tall dark girl stood against the wall on the stairs to let her pass.

Mrs Hubbard sighed and went on up.

Len Bateson said, 'What is it, Valerie? Complaints about our behaviour?'

'I don't know.' The girl came down the stairs. 'This place gets more like a madhouse every day.' She went through the door on the right.

In fact, 26 Hickory Road was two houses: 24 and 26. They had been made into one on the ground floor so that there was a large sitting room and dining room there. Two staircases led to the floors above which remained separate. The girls occupied bedrooms on the right-hand side of the house, and the men on the other, the original Number 24.

Upstairs, Mrs Hubbard knocked on the door of Mrs Nicoletis's room and entered. Mrs Nicoletis was on the sofa. She was a big woman, still good-looking, with an angry-looking mouth and large brown eyes.

'Ah! So there you are.'

'Yes,' said Mrs Hubbard, 'I was told you wanted to see me.'

'Yes, I do. It is disgusting!'

'What's disgusting?'

'These bills!' Mrs Nicoletis showed her a handful of papers. 'What are we feeding these students on? Shellfish and champagne? Is this the Ritz Hotel?'

'They get a good breakfast and a good evening meal – plain, healthy food. It is all very economical.'

'Economical? You dare to say that to me? When I am being ruined?'

'You make a very good profit, Mrs Nicoletis.'

'Bah! That Italian cook and her husband. They cheat you over the food.'

'Oh no, they don't. I can tell that no one cheats *me* over anything.'

'Then it is you yourself – you who are robbing me.'

Mrs Hubbard remained calm. 'I can't allow you to say things like that. It is not nice, and one day you will be in trouble for it.'

'Ah!' Mrs Nicoletis threw the bills up in the air from where they fell to the floor in all directions. 'You admit that these totals are higher than those of last week?'

'Of course they are.' Mrs Hubbard bent and picked the bills up. 'There's been some very good cut-price food at Lampson's Stores. I've taken advantage of it. Next week's totals will be below average. There.' Mrs Hubbard put the bills in a neat pile on the table. 'Anything else?'

'The American girl, Sally Finch, she talks of leaving – I do not want her to go. She will bring here other American scholars. She must not leave.'

'What's her reason for leaving?'

'How can I remember? It was not true, what she said. I could tell *that*. You will talk to her?'

'Yes, of course.'

'It must be because of the Communists – you know how Americans hate Communists. Nigel Chapman – *he* is a Communist.'

'I doubt it.'

'Yes, yes. You should have heard what he was saying one evening.'

'Nigel will say anything to annoy people.'

'You know them all so well. Dear Mrs Hubbard, you are wonderful! I say to myself again and again – what would I do without Mrs Hubbard?'

'Well, I'll do what I can.' She left the room and hurried along the passage to her own sitting room.

But there was to be no peace for Mrs Hubbard just yet. As she entered, a tall figure stood up and said, 'I would like to speak to you for a few minutes, please.'

'Of course, Elizabeth.'

Mrs Hubbard was rather surprised. Elizabeth Johnston was a girl from the West Indies who was studying Law. She was hard-working and ambitious, and kept herself to herself, but Mrs Hubbard heard a slight shake in her voice.

'Will you come with me to my room, please?'

Mrs Hubbard followed her up to the top floor. Elizabeth opened the door of her room and went across to a table near the window.

'Here are my work notes. The result of several months' hard study. You see what has been done?'

Mrs Hubbard gasped. Ink had been spilled on the table. It had run all over the papers. Mrs Hubbard touched it with her finger. It was still wet.

'This was done while I was out. It is not even my own ink. Somebody brought ink here and did it deliberately.'

'What a very cruel thing to do. Elizabeth, I am shocked and will do my best to find out who did this. Do you have any ideas about that?'

The girl replied at once. 'This is green ink. Not many people use it, but I know one person here who does. Nigel Chapman.'

'Nigel? Do you think Nigel would do a thing like that?'

'I don't think so – no.'

'Well, I'm very sorry, Elizabeth, that such a thing has happened in this house.'

'Thank you, Mrs Hubbard. There have been – other things, haven't there?'

'Yes – er – yes.'

Mrs Hubbard left the room and started towards the stairs. But she stopped suddenly and instead went along the passage to a door at the end. She knocked and a voice told her to enter. The room was a pleasant one and Sally Finch herself, a cheerful redhead, was a pleasant person. She was writing at a desk and looked up, smiling.

'Sally, have you heard what's happened to Elizabeth Johnston?'

'What has happened to her?'

Mrs Hubbard told her about the green ink.

'That's an awful thing to do,' Sally said. 'But everybody likes Elizabeth, so who . . . ? Well, it fits in with all the other things. That's why – '

'That's why what?'

Sally said slowly, 'That's why I'm getting out of here. Did Mrs Nick tell you?'

'Yes. She was very upset about it.'

'Well, I just don't like what's going on. It was strange losing my shoe, but then Valerie's scarf being all cut to bits and Len's rucksack . . . I've a feeling that there's a person in this house who isn't *right*.'

Mrs Hubbard went downstairs to the students' common room. There were four people there: Valerie Hobhouse, lying on a sofa; Nigel Chapman, sitting at a table with a heavy book open in front of him; Patricia Lane, leaning against the fireplace; and a girl in a coat, who was pulling off a woollen hat. She was a short, fair girl with brown eyes and a mouth that was usually a little open so that she always looked surprised.

'Something very unpleasant has happened,' Mrs Hubbard said. 'Nigel, I want you to help me.'

'Me, Madam?' Nigel shut his book. His thin face suddenly lit up with a surprisingly sweet smile. 'What have I done?'

'Nothing, I hope,' said Mrs Hubbard. 'But ink has been deliberately spilt all over Elizabeth Johnston's notes, and it's green ink.'

His smile disappeared. 'I use green ink.'

'Awful stuff,' said Patricia. 'I wish you wouldn't, Nigel.'

'I like being unusual,' said Nigel. 'But are you serious, Mum? About Elizabeth's papers?'

'Yes, I *am* serious. Did you do it, Nigel?'

'No, of course not. I like annoying people, but I would never do an unpleasant thing like that – and certainly not to Elizabeth. I usually keep my ink on the shelf over there.' He got up and went across the room. 'The bottle's nearly empty. It should be nearly full.'

The girl in the coat gasped. 'Oh, I don't like it – '

Nigel turned to her. 'Have you got an alibi, Celia?'

'I didn't do it. I really didn't. I've been at the hospital all day. I couldn't – '

'Now, Nigel,' said Mrs Hubbard. 'Don't joke with Celia.'

Patricia Lane said angrily, 'Why do you suspect Nigel? Just because *his* ink was taken – '

Valerie said, 'That's right, darling, defend your little boy. You know,' she looked at Mrs Hubbard, 'all this is getting beyond a joke. Something will have to be done about it.'

'Something is going to be done,' said Mrs Hubbard firmly.

Chapter 4

'Here you are, Monsieur Poirot.' Miss Lemon laid a small brown paper package before him. He removed the paper and looked at a silver evening shoe.

'It was at the Lost Property Office, just as you said.'

'That tells us my ideas are correct,' said Poirot.

'And I received a letter from my sister. There have been some new developments.' She handed it to him and, after reading it, he asked Miss Lemon to get her sister on the telephone.

'Oh, Monsieur Poirot, how kind of you to ring me up so quickly.'

'Mrs Hubbard, do you sometimes arrange talks at the hostel, or films?'

'Yes, sometimes.'

'Ah. Then this evening you will have persuaded Monsieur Hercule Poirot to come and talk to your students about his more interesting cases.'

Dinner was at seven-thirty and most of the students were already seated when Mrs Hubbard came down from her sitting room, followed by a small man with surprisingly black hair and a very large moustache.

'This is Monsieur Hercule Poirot who is kindly going to talk to us after dinner.'

Poirot sat down by Mrs Hubbard and busied himself with keeping his moustache out of the excellent soup which was served by an Italian manservant. This was followed by spaghetti and it was then that a girl sitting on Poirot's right spoke to him.

'Is it true that Mrs Hubbard's sister works for you?'

'But yes. Miss Lemon is the most perfect secretary that ever lived. I am sometimes afraid of her.'

'Oh I see. I wondered – '

'Now what did you wonder, *Mademoiselle*?' He smiled upon her in fatherly fashion, making a note in his mind as he did so: *'Pretty, worried, not very clever, frightened . . . '* He said, 'May I know your name and what it is you are studying?'

'Celia Austin. I don't study. I'm a chemist at St Catherine's Hospital.'

'And these others? Can you tell me something about them, perhaps?'

'Well, sitting on Mrs Hubbard's left is Nigel Chapman. He's studying Italian at London University. Then there's Patricia Lane, with glasses on, next to him. She's studying History. The big red-headed boy is Len Bateson, he's a medical student, and the dark girl is Valerie Hobhouse, she works in a beauty shop. Next to her is Colin McNabb – he's studying Psychology.' There was a change in her voice as she described Colin and her face went slightly pink.

Poirot said to himself, 'So – she is in love.' He noticed that McNabb never looked at her, as he was much too interested in his conversation with a laughing red-headed girl beside him.

'That's Sally Finch. She's American – studying Science. Then there's Geneviève Maricaud. She's doing English, and the small fair girl is Jean Tomlinson – she's at the hospital too, a physiotherapist. The black man is Akibombo – he comes from West Africa and he's very nice. Then there's Elizabeth Johnston, she's from Jamaica and she's studying Law.'

'Thank you. Do you all get on well together? Or do you have quarrels?' Poirot asked lightly.

Celia said, 'Oh, we're all too busy to have quarrels – although – '

'Although what, Miss Austin?'

'Well – Nigel – he likes making people angry. And Len Bateson *gets* angry. But he's very sweet really.'

'And Colin McNabb – does he too get annoyed?'

'Oh no. Colin just looks amused.'

'I see. And the young ladies, do you have your quarrels?'

'No, we all get on very well. Geneviève sometimes . . . I think French people can be a bit difficult – oh, I'm sorry – ' Celia looked confused.

'Me, I am Belgian,' said Poirot, and continued. 'What did you mean just now when you said that you wondered. You wondered – what?'

'Oh that – just, there have been some silly jokes lately – I thought Mrs Hubbard perhaps – no, I didn't mean anything.'

Poirot did not put pressure on her. He turned to Mrs Hubbard and was soon having a conversation with her and Nigel Chapman, who declared that crime was a form of creative art – and that people only became policemen to express their secret cruelty.

'All you young people nowadays think of nothing but politics and psychology,' Mrs Hubbard said. 'When I was a girl we used to dance, but you never do.'

Patricia Lane said, 'You see, Mrs Hubbard, with lectures to attend and then notes to write up, there's really not time for anything else.'

A chocolate pudding followed the spaghetti and afterwards they all went into the common room, and Poirot was invited to begin his talk. He spoke in his usual confident way about some of his more entertaining cases, exaggerating a little to amuse his audience. 'And so, you see,' he finished, 'prevention, always, is better than cure. We want to prevent murders – not wait until they have been committed.'

The students clapped loudly. Poirot bowed. And then, as he was about to sit down, Colin McNabb said, 'And now, perhaps, you'll talk about what you're really here for!'

Patricia said, 'Colin!'

'Well, we can guess, can't we?' He looked round. 'Monsieur Poirot has given us a very amusing little talk, but that's not what he came here for. He's here as a working detective. You don't really think, Monsieur Poirot, that we don't know *that*?'

'I will admit,' Poirot said, 'that Mrs Hubbard has told me that certain events have caused her – worry.'

Celia gave a frightened gasp. 'Then I *was* right!'

Mrs Hubbard spoke firmly. 'I asked Monsieur Poirot to give us a talk, but I also wanted to ask his advice about various things that have happened lately. Something has got to be done and it seemed to me that the only other possibility was – the police.'

At once a violent argument broke out and then, in a moment of quiet, Leonard Bateson's voice could be heard. 'Let's hear what Monsieur Poirot has to say about these troubles.'

Poirot bowed. 'Thank you.' As though performing a magic trick he brought out a pair of evening shoes and handed them to Sally Finch. 'Your shoes, *Mademoiselle*?'

'*Both* of them? Where did the missing one come from?'

'From the Lost Property Office at Baker Street Station.'

'But why did you think it might be there, Monsieur Poirot?'

'Someone takes a shoe from your room. Why? Not to wear and not to sell. And since everyone will try to find it, then the shoe must be got out of the house, or destroyed. But it is not so easy to destroy a shoe. The easiest way is to take it on a bus and leave it under a seat.' He paused. 'Monsieur Bateson has asked me to say what I myself think of these troubles. But it would not be right for me to speak unless I am invited to by all of you.'

'Oh, goodness,' Sally Finch said. 'This is a kind of party, all friends together. Let's hear what Monsieur Poirot advises without any more fuss.'

'I couldn't agree with you more, Sally,' said Nigel.

'Very well,' Poirot said. 'My advice is simple. Mrs Hubbard – or Mrs Nicoletis rather – should call in the police *at once*.'

Chapter 5

There was no doubt that Poirot's statement was unexpected. It caused a sudden and uncomfortable silence. Then Poirot was taken by Mrs Hubbard up to her sitting room. 'You are probably right,' she said. 'Perhaps we *should* get the police in – especially after this cruel ink business. But I wish you hadn't said so – right out like that.'

'Ah,' said Poirot. 'You think I should have kept it a secret?'

'Well, whoever has been doing these stupid things – well, that person is warned now.'

'Perhaps, yes.'

'Even if he's someone who wasn't here this evening, he will hear about it.'

'That is true.'

'And we can't call in the police unless Mrs Nicoletis agrees – oh, who's that now?' There had been a sharp knock on the door. Mrs Hubbard called crossly, 'Come in.'

Colin McNabb entered. 'Excuse me, but I would like to speak to you with Monsieur Poirot here.'

'With me?' Poirot turned his head in innocent surprise.

'Yes, with you.' Colin spoke sharply. 'I know you're a man who's had a lot of experience, but if you'll excuse me for saying so, your methods and your ideas are both very old-fashioned.'

'Really, Colin,' said Mrs Hubbard. 'You are extremely rude.'

'Crime and punishment, Monsieur Poirot – that's all you think about. But nowadays, even the Law has to understand that it is the *causes* that are important.'

'But there,' cried Poirot, 'I could not agree with you more!'

'Because there always is a reason, and it may be, to the person concerned, a very good reason. I am studying Psychology and what I'm saying is that you've got to understand the basic cause of the trouble if you're ever to cure the young criminal.'

Poirot said, 'I am willing to listen to you, Mr McNabb.'

Colin looked surprised. 'Thank you. Well, I'll start with the pair of shoes you returned to Sally Finch. Remember, *one* shoe was stolen. Only one.'

'I remember noticing the fact,' said Poirot.

Colin McNabb leaned forward. 'Ah, but you didn't see the *importance* of it. We have here, very definitely, a *Cinderella complex*. You know the Cinderella fairy story?'

'A French story – yes.'

'Cinderella, the servant, sits by the fire; her sisters go to the Prince's party. A fairy godmother sends Cinderella too, to that party. At midnight, her beautiful clothes turn back to rags – she escapes, leaving behind her *one shoe*. So here we have a mind that compares itself to Cinderella – the girl who steals a shoe. Why?'

'A girl?'

'Of course, a girl. That should be clear to the lowest intelligence.'

'Really, Colin!' said Mrs Hubbard.

'She wants to be the Princess, to be claimed by the Prince. Another important fact, the shoe is stolen from an attractive girl *who is going to a party*. So now let's look at a few of the other things that were taken. A powder compact, lipsticks, earrings, a bracelet, a ring – all pretty things, and there are two important points here. The girl wants to be *noticed*. And she also wants to be *punished*. It is not the *value* of these things that is wanted.'

'Yet a diamond ring was amongst the things stolen,' said Poirot.

'That was returned.'

'And surely, Mr McNabb, you would not say that a stethoscope is a pretty thing?'

'That had a deeper meaning. Women who feel they are not attractive can find confidence through professional work.'

'And the cookery book?'

'A symbol of home life, husband and family.'

'And boracic powder?'

Colin said crossly, 'Monsieur Poirot, *nobody* would steal boracic powder! Why would they?'

'This is what I have asked myself. Mr McNabb, you seem to have an answer for everything. Explain to me, then, the importance of an old pair of grey trousers – *your* trousers, I understand.'

For the first time Colin appeared uncomfortable. 'I could explain that – but it would be complicated, and perhaps –well, rather embarrassing.'

'Ah. And the ink that is spilt over another student's papers, the silk scarf that is cut. Do these things cause you no worry?'

Colin's calmness suddenly disappeared. 'They do. She ought to have treatment – *at once. Medical* treatment. She's all confused. If I . . .'

Poirot interrupted him. 'You know then who she is?'

'I think perhaps that I do.'

Poirot said quietly, 'A girl who is not very successful with men. A kind girl. A girl who is not very clever. A girl who feels lonely. A girl . . .'

There was a knock on the door.

'Come in,' said Mrs Hubbard.

The door opened.

'Ah,' said Poirot. 'Exactly. Miss Celia Austin.'

Celia looked at Colin with pain in her eyes. 'I didn't know you were here. I came because – ' She took a deep breath and rushed to

Mrs Hubbard. 'Please, please don't send for the police. It's me. I've been taking those things. I don't know why. I just – something told me to.' She turned to Colin. 'So now you know what I'm like . . . and you'll never speak to me again. I'm awful . . .'

'No you're not,' said Colin. 'If you'll trust me, Celia, I'll soon be able to put you right.'

'Oh Colin – really?'

He took her hand. 'Don't worry.' Then he looked at Mrs Hubbard. 'I hope now, that you will not call in the police. Celia will return anything she has taken.'

'I can't return the bracelet and the powder compact,' said Celia anxiously. 'I put them in a rubbish bin. But I'll buy new ones.'

'And the stethoscope?' said Poirot. 'Where did you put that?'

'I didn't take the stethoscope. And it wasn't me who spilt ink over Elizabeth's papers. I would never do a thing like that.'

'Yet you cut up Miss Hobhouse's scarf, *Mademoiselle*?'

Celia looked uncomfortable. 'That was different. I mean – Valerie didn't mind.'

'And the rucksack?'

'Oh, I didn't cut that up. That was done with anger.'

Poirot took out the list he had copied from Mrs Hubbard's notebook. 'Tell me, which of these things you did, or did not, take?'

Celia read the list. 'I don't know anything about the rucksack, or the electric light bulbs, or bath salts, and the ring was just a mistake. When I realised it was valuable I returned it.'

Colin said quickly. 'I can promise you that there will be no more things taken. From now on I'll be responsible for her.'

'Oh, Colin, you *are* good to me.'

'I would like you to tell me all about your early home life, Celia. Did your parents get on well together?'

'Oh no, it was *awful* – '

'Exactly. And – '

Mrs Hubbard interrupted. 'That is enough. I'm glad, Celia, that you've told the truth. Now, please go.' As the door closed behind them, she took a deep breath. 'Well, what do you think of that?'

Hercule Poirot smiled. 'I think – that we have helped at a love scene – modern style. In my young days love was all like a beautiful dream. Nowadays it is the difficulties which bring a boy and girl together.'

'All such nonsense,' said Mrs Hubbard. 'Celia's father died when she was young, but she had a very happy childhood.'

'Ah, but she is wise enough not to say so to young McNabb!'

'Do you believe all those ideas of his, Monsieur Poirot?'

'I do not believe that Celia had a Cinderella complex. I think she stole unimportant articles in order to attract the attention of Colin McNabb – and she has been successful.'

'I do apologize for wasting your time over such a silly business. Anyway, all's well that ends well.'

'No, no.' Poirot shook his head. 'I do not think we are at the end yet. There are things still that are not explained; and me, I think that we have here something serious – really serious. I wonder, *Madame*, if I could speak to Miss Patricia Lane. I would like to examine the ring that was stolen.'

'Why, of course, Monsieur Poirot. I'll go down and send her up to you.'

Patricia Lane came in shortly afterwards. 'Mrs Hubbard said you wanted to see my ring.' She slipped it off her finger and held it out to him. 'It was my mother's engagement ring.'

Poirot nodded. 'She is alive still, your mother?'

'No. Both my parents are dead.'

'That is sad.'

'Yes. They were both very nice people, but somehow I was never quite so close to them as I ought to have been. One feels sad about that afterwards. My mother wanted a daughter who was fond of clothes and parties. She was very disappointed that I preferred History.'

'You have always had a serious mind?'

'I think so. I feel that life is so short, I ought to be doing something important.'

Poirot looked at her thoughtfully. Apart from a little lipstick, Patricia Lane wore no make-up. Her mouse-coloured hair was combed back from her face and her blue eyes looked back at him through glasses.

Patricia was saying, 'I'm really very shocked about what happened to Elizabeth. It seems to me that someone deliberately used the green ink to blame Nigel. But Nigel would never do a thing like that.'

'Ah.' Poirot looked at her with more interest.

'Nigel's not easy to understand. You see, he had a very difficult home life.'

'My goodness, another of them!'

'What did you say?'

'Nothing. Please continue – '

'About Nigel. He's very clever, but even if everybody in this place thinks he did that trick with the ink, he won't say that he didn't. He'll just say, "Let them think it if they want to." And that attitude is really so stupid.'

'It can be misunderstood, certainly.'

'It's a kind of pride, I think. Because he has always been misunderstood. In some ways, in spite of his being so independent, he needs looking after like a child.'

Poirot felt, suddenly, very tired of love and was glad to be past all that. He stood up. 'Will you permit me, *Mademoiselle*, to keep your ring? It will be returned to you tomorrow.'

'Certainly,' said Patricia.

'And please, *Mademoiselle*, be careful.'

'Careful? Careful of what?'

'I wish I knew,' said Hercule Poirot.

Chapter 6

The next day Mrs Hubbard woke with a sense of relief. A silly girl had been responsible for the recent events. And now there was order again. Going down to breakfast, however, her new sense of peace was destroyed.

'Is it true, Ma?' said Len Bateson. 'That it's Celia who's been taking those things? Is that why she was not at breakfast?'

'I'm not really surprised,' said Sally. 'I always had a sort of idea . . .'

'Are you saying that it was Celia who threw ink on my notes?' Elizabeth looked shocked.

'Celia did *not* throw ink on your work,' said Mrs Hubbard. 'And I wish you would all stop discussing this. I meant to tell you all later, but – '

'But Jean was listening outside the door last night,' said Valerie.

'I was not listening. I just happened to go – '

'Come now, Elizabeth,' said Nigel. 'You know very well who threw the green ink. I did, of course.'

'He didn't!' said Patricia. 'He's only pretending. Nigel, how can you be so stupid?'

'I'm being kind to you, Pat. Who borrowed my ink yesterday morning? *You* did.'

'I do not understand, please,' said Mr Akibombo.

'You don't want to,' Sally said.

Colin McNabb had been trying to speak for some time. Now he hit the table hard with his hand and suddenly everyone was silent. 'Don't any of you know anything about psychology? Celia's been going through a very difficult time and she needs treating with kindness, not all this nonsense.'

'I quite agree about being *kind*,' said Jean, 'but we should not encourage stealing.'

'This wasn't *stealing*.' said Colin. 'You make me sick – all of you.'

'Interesting case, is she, Colin?' said Valerie, and smiled at him.

'If you're interested in the workings of the mind, yes.'

'I would like to make a formal protest,' said Mr Chandra Lal, an Indian student who also lived in the hostel. 'Boracic powder, very necessary for my eyes, was taken.'

'Please,' said Mr Akibombo. 'I still do not understand.'

'Come along,' said Sally. 'I'll tell you about it on the way to the college.' She guided him out of the room and was followed by the other students.

'Oh dear,' said Mrs Hubbard. 'Why did I ever take this job on?'

Valerie, who was the only person left, smiled. 'Don't worry, Ma. It's a good thing it's all come out. Everyone was getting very anxious.'

'I must say I was very surprised.'

'That it was Celia? I thought it was rather obvious, really.'

'Have you always thought that?'

'Well, one or two things made me wonder. Anyway, she's got Colin where she wants him.'

As Valerie went out, Mrs Hubbard heard her saying cheerfully in the hall, 'Good morning, Celia. All is known and all is going to be forgiven.'

Celia came into the dining room, her eyes red from crying.

'You're very late.' Mrs Hubbard said. 'The coffee's cold and there's not much left to eat.'

'I didn't want to meet the others.'

'You've got to meet them sooner or later.'

'Oh, I know, but of course I'll leave at the end of the week.'

'You don't need to do that. But you'll have to pay for anything that you can't return.'

Celia interrupted her eagerly. 'Oh, yes, I've got my cheque book with me.' It was in her hand with an envelope. 'And I had written to you in case you weren't here, to say how sorry I was.'

'All right.' Mrs Hubbard looked at the list of objects. 'It's difficult to say how much – '

'Well let me give you a cheque for what you think and then I can take some back or give you more later.'

Mrs Hubbard suggested a sum and Celia opened the cheque book and started to write, then stopped. 'Oh dear, my pen has no ink.' She went over to the shelves where there were various small things that belonged to the students. 'There isn't any ink here either, except Nigel's awful green. Oh, I'll use that.' She filled the pen and wrote out the cheque. Then she looked at her watch. 'I shall be late. I had better not stop for breakfast.'

'Now, you should have something, Celia – Yes, what is it?'

Geronimo, the Italian manservant, had come into the room. 'Mrs Nicoletis, she has just come in. She wants to see you. She is very angry.'

'I'm coming.' Mrs Hubbard left the room while Celia began cutting off a piece of bread.

Mrs Nicoletis was walking up and down her room and turned when she heard Mrs Hubbard come in. 'You sent for the police? Without a word to me? Who do you think you are?'

'I did not send for the police.'

'You are not telling the truth.'

'Mrs Nicoletis, you can't talk to me like that.'

'Oh no! Of course it is *I* who am wrong. Not *you*. Always *me*. Everything *you* do is perfect. Police in my respectable hostel.'

'But no one has "called in the police". A famous private detective had dinner here last night. He gave a very interesting talk to the students.'

'Yes, and you told this detective friend of yours all about our most private matters. That is a great breaking of trust.'

'Not at all. I'm responsible for this place and I'm glad to tell you that one of the students has admitted that she has been responsible for most of these things.'

'What is the good of that? My beautiful Students' Home will now have a bad name. No one will come.' Mrs Nicoletis sat down on the sofa and began to cry. 'Nobody thinks of my feelings. If I died tomorrow, who would care?'

Wisely leaving this question unanswered, Mrs Hubbard left the room.

She then put notes in all the students' rooms explaining that Celia wished to pay them for anything they had lost.

As she came down to dinner, Len Bateson stopped her. 'I'll wait for Celia out in the hall, and bring her in. So that she knows everything is all right.'

'That's very nice of you, Len.'

So, as soup was being passed round, Len's voice was heard from the hall. 'Come along in, Celia. All friends here.'

Nigel remarked sharply to his soup plate, 'So, he's done *his* good job for the day!' but he waved to Celia as she came in with Len's arm round her. And there was a general sound of cheerful conversation.

Colin McNabb came in late and seemed quieter than usual. When the meal was nearly finished he got up and said, 'I've got to go out and see someone, but I would like to tell you all first.

Celia and I – hope to get married next year when I've done my course.' He immediately received good wishes and jokes from his friends and finally escaped.

'I'm so glad, Celia,' said Patricia. 'I hope you'll be very happy.'

'Everything is now perfect,' said Nigel. 'Why is dear Jean looking so serious? Do you disapprove of marriage, Jean?'

'Of course not.'

'I always think it's so *much* better than free love, don't you? Nicer for the children. Looks better on their passports.'

Elizabeth Johnston said suddenly, 'I would still like to talk about what happened yesterday.'

Valerie said, 'What's the matter, Elizabeth?'

'Oh, please,' said Celia. 'I really think that if the person who threw the ink on your papers, and cut up that rucksack, admits it like I've done, then everything will be all right.'

Valerie said with a short laugh, 'And we'll all live happily ever after.'

They all got up and went into the common room. There was some competition to give Celia her coffee, then finally everyone living in 24 and 26 Hickory Road went to bed.

Chapter 7

Miss Lemon was rarely, if ever, late. Storms, illness, transport failure – none of these things seemed to affect her. But this morning Miss Lemon arrived, breathless, at five minutes past ten instead of at ten o'clock.

'I'm extremely sorry, Monsieur Poirot. I was just about to leave the flat when my sister rang up, very upset. One of the students has committed suicide.'

'What is the name of the student?'

'A girl called Celia Austin.'

'How?'

'They think she took morphia.'

'Could it have been an accident?'

'Oh no. She left a note.'

Poirot said softly, 'It was not this I expected, no, . . . and yet it is true, I expected *something*.' He looked at Miss Lemon. 'Please answer what letters you can. Me, I will go round to Hickory Road.'

Geronimo let Poirot in. 'Sir, we have here big trouble. The girl, she is dead in her bed this morning. First the doctor came. Now comes an Inspector of the police. He is upstairs with Mrs Hubbard. Why would she wish to kill herself, when last night she was engaged to be married?'

'Engaged?'

'Yes, yes, to Mr Colin.' Geronimo opened the door of the common room for Poirot. 'You stay here, yes? When the police go, I will tell Mrs Hubbard you are here.'

Upstairs, Mrs Hubbard was with Inspector Sharpe, who was asking questions. He was a big, comfortable-looking man with a gentle manner that hid his determination.

'There will have to be an inquest,' he said. 'So we must get the facts right. Now, this girl had been unhappy lately, you say?'

'Yes.'

'Love affair?'

'Not exactly.' Mrs Hubbard paused.

'You think perhaps she had a reason for killing herself?'

'Inspector Sharpe, the girl had done some very stupid things, but . . .'

'Yes?'

'Well, for three months things have been disappearing – small things, I mean – nothing important. No money.'

'And this girl was responsible?'

'Yes. The night before last a friend of mine came to dinner. A Monsieur Hercule Poirot – perhaps you know the name?'

Inspector Sharpe's eyes opened rather wide. 'Monsieur Hercule Poirot? Now that's very interesting.'

'He gave us a little talk after dinner and we discussed the fact that things had been stolen. He advised me, in front of them all, to go to the police.'

'He did, did he?'

'Afterwards, Celia came to my room and admitted everything. She was very upset.'

'Were you going to tell the police?'

'No. She was going to pay for everything, and everyone was very nice to her about it.'

'Was she short of money?'

'No. She had a job as a pharmacist at St Catherine's Hospital and a little money of her own. It was kleptomania, I suppose,' said Mrs Hubbard. 'You see, there was a young man she was fond of.'

'And he ended their relationship?'

'Oh no. The *complete* opposite. He defended her very strongly, and last night he told us that they were now engaged to be married.'

Inspector Sharpe looked very surprised. 'And then she goes to bed and takes morphia?'

'I can't understand it.' Mrs Hubbard shook her head.

'And yet the facts are clear.' Sharpe looked at the small, torn piece of paper on the table.

Dear Mrs Hubbard, I really am sorry and this is the best thing I can do.

'It's not signed, but you are sure it's her handwriting?'

'Yes.' But Mrs Hubbard was worried. Why did she feel so strongly that there was something *wrong* about it?

'There's one clear fingerprint on it which is definitely hers,' said the Inspector. 'The morphia was in a small bottle with the label of St Catherine's Hospital on it, so she probably brought it home with her yesterday in order to commit suicide.'

'I really can't believe that. She was so happy last night.'

'Well, perhaps her mood changed when she went up to bed. Perhaps there was more in her past than you know about. This young man of hers – what's his name?'

'Colin McNabb. He's doing a Psychology course at St Catherine's. Celia was very much in love with him, more, I think, than he was with her.'

'That probably explains things. She hadn't told him everything she should have. Young people are very romantic and sometimes expect too much of love affairs.' He stood up. 'Thank you, Mrs Hubbard. Her mother died two years ago and the only relative is an elderly aunt – we'll contact her.' He picked up the small piece of paper with Celia's writing on it.

'There's something wrong about that,' said Mrs Hubbard suddenly.

'Wrong? In what way?'

'I don't know – but I feel I should know. Oh dear, I feel so stupid this morning.'

'It's all been very difficult for you.' Inspector Sharpe opened the door and immediately fell over Geronimo, who was pressed against it. 'Hello,' he said. 'Listening at doors, eh?'

'No, no, I do not listen – never! I am just coming in with message.'

'I *see.* What message?'

'There is gentleman downstairs to see Mrs Hubbard.'

'All right. Go in and tell her.'

The Inspector walked down the passage and then paused as he heard Geronimo say, 'The gentleman with the moustache, he is waiting to see you.'

'Gentleman with the moustache, eh,' said Sharpe to himself, and went downstairs and into the common room. 'Hello, Monsieur Poirot. It's a long time since we met.'

Calmly Poirot turned from where he had been examining a bookshelf near the fireplace. 'Surely – yes, it is Inspector Sharpe, is it not? But you did not work in this part of London?'

'I moved here two years ago. So I would like to know *why* you came along here the other night to give a talk on criminology to students.'

Poirot smiled. 'But Mrs Hubbard here is the sister of my wonderful secretary, Miss Lemon. So when she asked me – '

'When she asked you to investigate what had been going on here, you came along. That's it really, isn't it?'

'You are correct.'

'But why? A silly girl taking a few things. Why did that interest you, Monsieur Poirot?'

Poirot shook his head. 'It is not so simple as that.'

'Why not? I don't understand,' Sharpe said.

'No, and I do not understand. The things that were taken – they did not make a pattern – they did not make sense. And other things happened that were meant to fit in with the pattern of Celia Austin – but they did *not* fit in. They were meaningless, and some were even cruel. But Celia was not cruel.'

'She was a kleptomaniac?'

'I very much doubt it. It is my opinion that stealing these cheap objects was to attract the attention of a certain young man.'

'Colin McNabb?'

'Yes. She was in love with Colin McNabb, who never noticed her. So instead of being a pretty, well-behaved girl, she became a young criminal. Colin McNabb was immediately interested in her.'

'He must be very stupid.'

'Not at all. He is a keen psychologist.'

'Oh, one of *those*! I understand now.' Inspector Sharpe smiled. 'So, the girl was rather clever.'

'Surprisingly so. And I think the idea had been suggested to her by someone else.'

'But still,' said Sharpe, 'I don't understand. If this kleptomania business was successful, why did she commit suicide?'

'The answer is that she did *not* commit suicide. Are you quite sure that she did?'

'It's obvious, Monsieur Poirot and – '

The door opened and Mrs Hubbard came in looking very pleased with herself. 'I've got it. It came to me suddenly. Why that suicide note looked wrong, I mean. Celia couldn't possibly have written it.'

'Why not, Mrs Hubbard?' asked Sharpe.

'Because it's written in blue-black ink. And Celia filled her pen with green ink – that ink over there – at breakfast time yesterday morning.' She went to the shelf and held up the nearly empty bottle. 'I am sure that the piece of paper was torn out of the letter she wrote to me yesterday – and which I never opened.'

'What did she do with it? Can you remember?'

Mrs Hubbard shook her head. 'I left her alone in here and she must have just forgotten about it.'

'And somebody found it and opened it . . . somebody – ' The Inspector paused. 'You understand what this means? Somebody saw the possibility of using the opening words of her letter to you – to suggest something very different. To suggest suicide – So this means – '

'Murder,' said Hercule Poirot.

Chapter 8

It was five o'clock and Inspector Sharpe was drinking his third cup of tea. 'Thank you for inviting me to your home, Monsieur Poirot. I've got an hour to wait until the students get back to the house so that I can question them all.'

'You have been to St Catherine's Hospital?' Poirot asked.

'Yes. The chief pharmacist was very helpful.'

'What did he say about the girl?'

'She had worked there for just over a year and everyone liked her.' He paused. 'The morphia certainly came from there.'

'It did? That is interesting – and rather strange.'

'It was morphine tartrate and was kept in the poison cupboard on the upper shelf, amongst drugs that were not often used.'

'So, if one small bottle disappeared it would not immediately be noticed?'

'That's right. The three pharmacists all had keys to the poison cupboard, but on a busy day someone is going to it every few minutes, therefore the cupboard is unlocked and remains unlocked till the end of work.'

'What outsiders come into the pharmacy?'

'Quite a lot of people go through the pharmacy to get to the chief pharmacist's office – and salesmen from big drug companies go through it too. Then, of course, friends come in sometimes to see one of the pharmacists.'

'Who came in recently to see Celia Austin?'

Sharpe looked at his notebook. 'A girl called Patricia Lane came on Tuesday last week. She wanted Celia to meet her at the cinema after the pharmacy closed.'

'Patricia Lane,' said Poirot thoughtfully.

'She was only there for about five minutes and did not go near the poison cupboard. They also remember a West Indian girl coming – about two weeks ago. She was interested in the work and asked questions about it and made notes.'

'That must be Elizabeth Johnston. Anyone else?'

'Not that the other pharmacists can remember.'

'Do doctors come to the pharmacy?'

Sharpe smiled. 'All the time. Sometimes to ask about a particular drug. Sometimes they just come in for a talk to the girls. And a lot of young fellows come in for pills because they've been drinking too much.'

Poirot said, 'And if I remember rightly, one or more of the students at Hickory Road is studying at St Catherine's – a big, red-haired boy – Bateman – '

'Leonard Bateson. That's right. And Colin McNabb is doing a course there. Then there's a girl, Jean Tomlinson, who works in the physiotherapy department.'

'And all of these have probably been quite often in the pharmacy?'

'Yes, and nobody remembers when because they're so used to seeing them.'

'It is not easy,' said Poirot.

'No, it is not!' Sharpe paused. 'You said this morning that someone might have suggested the kleptomania idea to Celia Austin. If so, who?'

'Only three of the students, I believe, would have been able to think of such an idea. Leonard Bateson might have suggested kleptomania to Celia almost as a joke, but I do not really think he would have allowed such a thing to go on for so long. Nigel Chapman is a humorous and slightly cruel character. He would think it good fun, and would not care if things went wrong.

The third person is a young woman called Valerie Hobhouse. She is clever and has probably read enough psychology to judge Colin's probable reaction.'

'Thanks,' said Sharpe, writing down the names. 'And is that all the help you can give me, Monsieur Poirot?'

'I fear so. But I shall continue to be interested and do what I can. For me, there is only one method.'

'And that is?'

'*Conversation*, my friend. Conversation and again conversation! All the murderers I have ever met enjoyed talking. They are so pleased with themselves that sooner or later they say something that shows they know too much about the crime.'

Sharpe stood up. 'I suppose every single one of the students is a possible murderer.'

'I think so,' said Poirot lightly.

Chapter 9

Inspector Sharpe leaned back in his chair and took a deep breath. He had interviewed a tearful French girl, the gentle Mr Akibombo and several other foreign students who did not really understand what he was saying. None of these, he was certain, knew anything about the death of Celia Austin.

His next interview was with Nigel Chapman, who immediately took control of the conversation. 'Of course, I had an idea that you'd got it wrong when you thought it was suicide. But it rather pleases me that you suddenly saw it in a new way because she filled her pen with my green ink. The one thing the murderer couldn't possibly have expected. I suppose you've thought carefully about what can be the motive for this crime?'

'I'm asking the questions, Mr Chapman,' said Inspector Sharpe.

'Oh, of course,' said Nigel. 'I was trying to go directly to the important points. But I suppose we've got to go through all the usual boring questions. Name, Nigel Chapman. Age, twenty-five. I'm studying History at London University. Anything else you want to know?'

'What is your home address, Mr Chapman?'

'No home address. I have a father, but he and I have quarrelled, and his address is therefore no longer mine. So 26 Hickory Road and Coutts Bank, will always find me.'

Inspector Sharpe did not react to Nigel's behaviour. He suspected that it hid his nervousness of being questioned about a murder. 'How well did you know Celia Austin?' he asked.

'I knew her very well in the sense that I saw her almost every day, but in fact I didn't *know* her at all. I wasn't interested in her and I think she probably disapproved of me.'

'Did she disapprove of you for any particular reason?'

'She didn't like my sense of humour.'

'When was the last time you saw Celia Austin?'

'At dinner yesterday evening. When Colin told us they were engaged.'

'Was that at dinner or in the common room?'

'At dinner. Afterwards, when we went into the common room, Colin went off somewhere.'

'And the rest of you had coffee in the common room?'

'Yes.'

'Did Celia Austin have coffee?'

'Well, I suppose so. I mean, I didn't actually notice her having coffee, but she must have had it.'

'You did not personally hand her some coffee?'

'Are you trying to suggest something, Mr Sharpe? Well, I didn't go near her. I've never been attracted to Celia, and her engagement to Colin McNabb caused no murderous feelings in me.'

'I'm not suggesting anything like that, Mr Chapman,' said Sharpe. 'But somebody wanted Celia Austin dead. Why?'

'I can't imagine why, Inspector. Celia was such a boring girl, but very nice, not at all the type to get herself murdered.'

'Were you surprised when you found that it was Celia who had been stealing things here?'

'Very.'

'You didn't, perhaps, encourage her to take those things?'

'Me! Why would I? And surely, Inspector, the reason was psychological?'

'Do you think that Celia Austin was a kleptomaniac?'

'What other explanation can there be?'

'You don't think that someone might have suggested it to Miss Austin as a way of – say – making Mr McNabb look at her in a new way?'

Nigel's eyes shone. 'Now that really is a most interesting explanation. And it's perfectly possible, because of course Colin would react like that.'

'Have you any ideas, Mr Chapman, about the things that have been going on in this house? About, for example, the throwing of ink over Miss Johnston's papers?'

'If you're thinking *I* did it, Inspector, that's quite untrue. Of course, it looks like me because of the green ink, but if you ask *me*, somebody used my ink to make it look like me.'

The next person on Inspector Sharpe's list was Leonard Bateson. He was even more uncomfortable than Nigel, though it showed in a different way.

'All right!' he shouted, after the first few questions. '*I* poured out Celia's coffee and gave it to her. And you can believe it or not, but there was no morphia in it.'

'You saw her drink it?'

'No. We were all moving around and I got into an argument with someone just after that.'

'So you are saying that *anybody* could have dropped morphia into her coffee cup?'

'No. You try to put anything in anyone's cup! Everybody would see you.'

'Would they?' said Sharpe.

Len shouted, 'Why do you think I would want to poison the girl? I liked her. She must have taken it herself. There's no other explanation.'

'We might think so, if it wasn't for the false suicide note.'

'False! She wrote it, didn't she?'

'She wrote it as part of a letter, early that morning.'

'Well – she could have torn a bit out and used it as a suicide note.'

'Really, Mr Bateson, if you wanted to write a suicide note you would write one. You wouldn't take a letter you had written to somebody else and carefully tear out one particular bit.'

'I might do. People do all sorts of strange things.'

'So did you believe Celia when she said she had stolen the things in the house?'

'Of course. But it did seem strange. She didn't seem to be the type to be a kleptomaniac. Nor a thief either.'

'And you can't think of any other reason for her having done it?'

'What other reason could there be?'

'Well, she might have wanted to make Colin McNabb interested in her.'

Len shook his head. 'She wouldn't have been able to plan a thing like that. She didn't have the knowledge.'

'*You've* got the knowledge, though, haven't you?'

Len gave a short laugh. 'You think I would do a stupid thing like that? You're mad.'

The Inspector changed direction. 'Do you think that Celia Austin spilled the ink over Elizabeth Johnston's papers, or do you think someone else did it?'

'Someone else. Celia said she didn't do that and I believe her. She never got annoyed with Elizabeth, not like some people did.'

'Who got annoyed with her – and why?'

'She criticised people, you know.' Len paused. 'Anyone who said something without really thinking. She would look across the table and say something like, "I'm afraid that is not proved by the facts. It has been well established by mathematics that . . ." Well, it was annoying – especially to Nigel, for example.'

'Ah yes. Nigel Chapman.'

'And it was green ink, too.'

'So you think it was Nigel who did it?'

'Well, it's possible.'

'Can you think of anybody else who Elizabeth Johnston annoyed?'

'Well, Colin McNabb wasn't too pleased now and again, nor was Jean Tomlinson.'

Sharpe saw Valerie Hobhouse next.

Valerie was cool and stylish. She seemed much less nervous than either of the men. She had been fond of Celia, she said. Celia was not very clever and it was rather sad the way she so loved Colin McNabb.

'Do you think she was a kleptomaniac, Miss Hobhouse?'

'Well, I suppose so. I don't really know much about the subject.'

'Do you think anyone had encouraged her to do what she did?'

'You mean in order to attract Colin?'

'You're very quick on the point, Miss Hobhouse. Yes, that's what I mean. You didn't suggest it to her, perhaps?'

Valerie smiled. 'Well, no, considering that a favourite scarf of mine was cut to pieces. I'm not as kind as that.'

'Do you think anyone else suggested it to her?'

'No. I think it was just natural behaviour.'

'What do you mean by natural?'

'Well, I first suspected that it was Celia when Sally's shoe went missing. Celia was jealous of Sally. She's easily the most attractive girl here and Colin gave her a lot of attention. So, on the night of this party, Sally's shoe disappeared and she had to go in an old black dress and black shoes. And there was Celia looking as pleased as a cat that's swallowed the cream. But I didn't suspect her of taking all these other things like bracelets and compacts.'

'Who did you think took those?'

Valerie shook her head. 'Oh, I don't know. One of the cleaning women, I thought.'

'And the rucksack that was cut up?'

'Was there a rucksack taken? I had forgotten.'

'Miss Hobhouse, have you any ideas of your own about Celia Austin's death? Any idea of the motive for it?'

Valerie's face was serious now. 'No. It was a horrible thing to happen. I can't think of anybody who wanted Celia to die. She was a nice girl and she had just got engaged, and . . .'

'And?'

'I wondered if that was why,' said Valerie slowly. 'Because she had got engaged. Because she was going to be happy. But that means somebody is – well – mad.'

Inspector Sharpe looked at her thoughtfully. 'Yes. Madness is a possible reason. So, have you any theory about the ink on Elizabeth Johnston's papers?'

'I don't believe that Celia would do a thing like that.'

'Any idea who it could have been?'

'Well . . . not a reasonable idea.'

'But an unreasonable one?'

'Well, I've got a sort of idea that it was Patricia Lane.'

'Really! Now you do surprise me. Patricia Lane seems such a well-balanced young lady.'

'I'm not saying she did do it. I just think she might have.'

'Why?'

'Well, Patricia disliked Elizabeth because she was always criticising her beloved Nigel. You know, when he made silly statements, the way he does.'

'You think it was more likely to have been Patricia rather than Nigel himself?'

'Oh, yes. Nigel wouldn't bother, and he would certainly not use his own special ink.'

'Then it might be somebody who did not like Nigel Chapman and wanted to make people think that he did it? Who does dislike him?'

'Oh, well, Jean Tomlinson does. And Nigel and Len Bateson often quarrel with each other.'

'Have you any ideas, Miss Hobhouse, how morphia could have been given to Celia Austin?'

'I suppose the coffee is the most obvious way. We were all moving around in the common room. Celia's coffee was on a small table near her and she always waited until it was nearly cold before she drank it. Anybody could have dropped a pill or something into her cup.'

'The morphia,' said Inspector Sharpe, 'was in the form of a powder.'

'Oh. That would be rather more difficult, wouldn't it?'

'Can you describe to me exactly what happened that evening in the common room?'

'Well, we all sat about, talked. Most of the boys went out. Celia went up to bed rather early and so did Jean Tomlinson. Sally and I stayed there rather late. I was writing letters and Sally was reading some notes. I think I was the last to go up to bed.'

'Thank you, Miss Hobhouse. Will you send Miss Lane to me now?'

Patricia Lane looked worried, but not frightened. And she told the Inspector nothing very new. When he asked her about Elizabeth Johnston's papers, Patricia said that she was sure that Celia had thrown the ink on them.

'But she said she didn't, Miss Lane.'

'Well, of course, she would. But it fits in, doesn't it, with all the other things?'

'Do you know what I think about this case, Miss Lane? That nothing fits in very well.'

'I suppose,' said Patricia, 'that you think it was Nigel who did it, because of the ink. That's such *nonsense.* I mean, Nigel wouldn't have used his own ink if he had done a thing like that. But anyway, he wouldn't do it.'

'He didn't always get on very well with Miss Johnston, did he?'

'Oh, she could be annoying sometimes, but he didn't really mind.' Patricia Lane leaned forward. 'I would like to try to make you understand some things about Nigel, Inspector. I'm the first to admit that he's got a very difficult manner. It turns people against him. He's rude and makes fun of people, but really he's very different from what he seems. He's one of those shy, rather unhappy people who really want to be liked, but who, for some reason, find themselves saying and doing the opposite to what they mean to say and do.'

'Ah,' said Inspector Sharpe. 'Rather unfortunate, that.'

'Yes, but it comes from having had an unfortunate childhood. Nigel's father was very hard and never understood him. He treated his mother very badly too. After she died they had a big quarrel and Nigel left the house, and his father said that he would never give him any help or money. Nigel said he didn't want anything from his father, and he never went near him again. Since his mother died, he's never had anyone to care for him. He has a wonderful mind, but just can't show himself as he really is.'

Inspector Sharpe looked at her thoughtfully. 'In love with the fellow,' he thought. He wondered if Nigel Chapman had been attracted to Celia Austin. If so, Patricia Lane might have disliked her a lot. Disliked her enough to murder her? Surely not – and of course, the fact that Celia had got engaged to Colin McNabb would surely destroy that as a possible motive. He thanked Patricia Lane and asked for Jean Tomlinson.

Chapter 10

Jean Tomlinson was a severe-looking young woman, with fair hair and a rather tight mouth. She sat down. 'How can I help you, Inspector? It was bad enough when we thought Celia had committed suicide, but now that it's supposed to be murder . . .' She stopped and shook her head.

'Do you know where the poison came from?' said Sharpe.

Jean nodded. 'I hear it came from St Catherine's Hospital, but that makes it seem more like suicide.'

'It was probably intended to. I hear that you often visited the pharmacy, Miss Tomlinson.'

'I went in there to see my friend Mildred, one of the other pharmacists, yes. But I would never have gone to the poison cupboard.'

'But you could have done so?'

'That is a disgusting accusation, Inspector Sharpe.'

'But it's not an accusation, Miss Tomlinson. I am just saying that it was *possible* for you to go to the poison cupboard. I'm not saying that you did so. I mean, why would you?'

'Exactly. I was a friend of Celia's.'

'People do sometimes get poisoned by their friends. Did you suspect it was Celia who had stolen the things in the house?'

'No. I always thought Celia had high principles.'

'Of course,' said Sharpe, 'kleptomaniacs can't really help themselves, can they?'

Jean Tomlinson paused. 'I can't agree with *that* idea. Stealing is stealing. People should be punished for these things.'

'But instead, everything was ending happily and Miss Austin was getting married.'

'One isn't surprised at anything Colin McNabb does,' said Jean. 'He isn't religious and my opinion is that he's a *Communist*! He supported Celia, because he thinks everyone should just take anything they want.'

'What about the ink on Elizabeth Johnston's papers? Did she do that?'

'It does seem unlikely.'

'You think it was Nigel Chapman?'

'No, I don't think Nigel would do that either. I think it was probably Mr Akibombo.'

'Really? Why would he do it?'

'Jealousy. Because Elizabeth is so clever.'

Inspector Sharpe thought for a moment. 'When was the last time you saw Celia Austin?'

'After dinner on Friday night.'

'Who went up to bed first, she or you?'

'I did.'

'And you've no idea who could have put morphia into her coffee – if it was given that way?'

'No idea at all.'

'You never saw morphia anywhere in the house?'

'No, I don't think so.'

'You don't *think* so, Miss Tomlinson?'

'Well, I just wondered. There was that silly bet.'

'What bet?'

'Oh, some of the boys were arguing – Colin and Nigel started it, and then Len joined in and Patricia was there too.'

'What were they arguing about?'

'Murder, and ways of doing it.'

'Really? Can you remember what was said?'

Jean Tomlinson considered. 'Well, it started with a discussion on murder by using poison. They said that the difficulty was to obtain the poison, that the murderer was usually found because of where he bought poison or because he had an opportunity to get it. But Nigel said that he could think of three ways by which anyone could obtain a poison, and nobody would ever know. Len Bateson said that he was talking nonsense. Nigel said no he wasn't, and he would prove it. Pat said that Nigel was right and that either Len or Colin could probably get poison any time they liked from a hospital, and so could Celia. And Nigel said that wasn't what he meant at all. He said that he, who wasn't a doctor or pharmacist, could get three different types of poison by three different methods. Len Bateson said, "All right, then, but what are your methods?" and Nigel said, "I won't tell you, now, but I bet you that within three weeks I can produce three deadly poisons here," and Len Bateson said he would bet him five pounds he couldn't do it.'

'Well, what happened?' said Inspector Sharpe.

'Nothing for some time and then, one evening in the common room, Nigel said, "Look here – I did it," and he put three things on the table: a tube of hyoscine pills, a bottle of digitalis, and a tiny bottle of morphine.'

The Inspector said sharply, 'Morphine. Any label on it?'

'Yes, it had St Catherine's Hospital on it.'

'And the others?'

'I don't think they were from hospitals.'

'What happened next?'

'Well, Len Bateson said, "But if you had committed a murder this would soon lead to you," and Nigel said, "No it wouldn't. I have no connection with any hospital and nobody will connect me with these." Well, they argued a bit but in the end Len said he would pay the five pounds. He then said, "What are we going to do with the poisons?" Nigel said we had better get rid of them before any accidents happened, so they threw the pills and the morphine on the fire. The digitalis they poured down the lavatory.'

'And the bottles?'

'I don't know what happened to the bottles.'

'And this all happened – when?'

'Just over two weeks ago, I think.'

Inspector Sharpe remained thinking for a while after she had gone. Then he asked Nigel Chapman in again. 'I've just had a rather interesting statement from Miss Tomlinson,' he said.

'Ah! Who's dear Jean been poisoning your mind against? Me?'

'She's been talking about poison, and in connection with you, Mr Chapman. I hear that you had a bet with Mr Bateson about three methods of obtaining poison?'

'Oh, that!' Nigel smiled. 'Yes, of course! I don't even remember Jean being there.'

'You admit it, then?'

'Oh yes. Colin and Len were being rather annoying so . . .'

'So what were your three methods, Mr Chapman?'

Nigel leant his head on one side. 'Aren't you asking me to incriminate myself?'

'You can refuse to answer my questions if you like.'

Nigel considered for a moment, a slight smile on his lips. 'Of course, what I did was against the law. You could charge me for it. But if it's got any connection with poor little Celia's death, I suppose I should tell you.'

'That would certainly be the sensible decision.'

'All right then, I'll talk.'

'What were these three methods?'

'Well.' Nigel leant back in his chair. 'One's always reading in the papers about doctors losing dangerous drugs from a car. So I thought that one very simple method would be to go down to the country, follow a doctor about and, when the opportunity came, just open the car, look in the doctor's case, and take what you wanted. I had to follow three doctors until I found a suitably careless one. When I did, it was so easy. The car was left outside a farmhouse. I looked in the case, took out a tube of hyoscine, and that was that.'

'And method number two?'

'That involved Celia, but she had no idea what I was doing. I just talked about the funny way doctors write prescriptions, and asked her to write one for me like a doctor would write it, for digitalis. So she did. All I then had to do was to find a doctor living in another part of London, write his signature on the prescription so that it was hard to read, and take it to a chemist in another busy part of London. I received the medicine without any difficulty at all.'

'And the third method?'

'I *am* incriminating myself! I can hear it in your voice.'

'Stealing drugs from an unlocked car is larceny. Forging a prescription . . .'

Nigel interrupted him. 'But I didn't obtain money by it, and it wasn't a copy of any particular doctor's signature. Anyway I'm only telling you because . . .'

'Yes, Mr Chapman . . . ?'

Nigel said with sudden feeling, 'Celia didn't deserve to be murdered and I want to help.'

'Mr Chapman, the police can choose how they treat some types of behaviour. So please, tell me about your third method.'

'Well,' said Nigel, 'it was a bit more risky than the other two, but it was also more fun. You see, I had been to visit Celia before in her pharmacy. I knew the place reasonably well . . .'

'So you were able to take the bottle out of the cupboard?'

'No, no, if I had been planning a *real* murder, someone would remember that I had been there. No, I knew that Celia always went into the back room at eleven-fifteen for a cup of coffee. There was a new girl there and she didn't know me, so with a white coat on and a stethoscope round my neck, I walked into the pharmacy when she was alone there. I went along to the poison cupboard, took out a bottle, then asked the girl if she had a couple of headache pills as I had had too much to drink the night before. I swallowed them and walked out. She never suspected that I wasn't a doctor. It was so easy.'

'A stethoscope,' said Inspector Sharpe. 'Where did you get that?'

Nigel smiled. 'It was Len Bateson's. You should have seen everyone's face when I put those three poisons on the table. But we got rid of all of them at least two weeks ago.'

'That is what you think, Mr Chapman, but it may not really be so.'

'What do you mean?'

'How long had you had these things in your possession?'

'Well, the hyoscine about ten days. The morphine, about four days. The digitalis I had only got that afternoon.'

'And where did you keep these things?'

'In my chest of drawers, under my socks.'

'Did anyone know that?'

'No.'

'Did you tell anyone about what you were doing?'

'No. At least – no, I didn't.'

'You said "at least", Mr Chapman.'

'Well, I was going to tell Pat, then I thought she wouldn't approve, so I didn't. I told her after I had got them. She was not amused. But we just threw it all on the fire and down the lavatory with no harm done.'

'But it's very possible that harm was done. Have you never thought, Mr Chapman, that someone might have seen where you put those things, and that someone might have emptied morphia out of the bottle and replaced it with something else?'

'Goodness no! But nobody could possibly have known.'

'Which students might normally go into your room?'

'Well, I share it with Len Bateson. Most of the men here have been in it. Not the girls, of course. They're not allowed to come to the bedroom floors on our side of the house.'

'But they might still do so?'

'Anyone *might*,' said Nigel. 'In the afternoon there's nobody about.'

'Does Miss Lane ever come to your room?'

'I hope you don't mean that the way it sounds, Inspector. Pat comes to my room sometimes to return some socks she's mended. That's all.'

Leaning forward, Inspector Sharpe said, 'You do see, Mr Chapman, that the person who could most easily have taken some of that poison out of the bottle, was yourself?'

Nigel looked at him, his face suddenly very tired. 'Yes. I saw that just a minute and a half ago. But I had no reason to kill the girl, Inspector, and I didn't do it. Although you've only got my word for it.'

Chapter 11

Len Bateson and Colin McNabb both agreed that the story of the bet and the throwing away of the poison was true. Sharpe kept Colin McNabb back after the others had gone.

'I don't want to cause you any more pain than I can help, Mr McNabb – '

'You need not concern yourself with my feelings,' said Colin, his face showing nothing. 'Just ask me any questions which you think may be useful to you.'

'It was your opinion that Celia Austin's behaviour had a psychological origin?'

'There's no doubt about it. Her childhood had been very difficult because . . .'

'Yes, I'm sure.' Inspector Sharpe did not want to hear the story of yet another unhappy childhood. Nigel's had been enough. 'You had been attracted to her for some time?'

'I would not say that,' said Colin. 'Subconsciously no doubt, but I was not aware of it.'

'Had Celia any enemies here?'

'No, Inspector. Celia was well liked. I do not think it was a personal matter, the reason she was killed.'

'What do you mean by "not a personal matter"?'

'I do not wish to say at the moment. I'm not clear about it myself.'

The Inspector could not move him from that position.

The last two students to be interviewed were Sally Finch and Elizabeth Johnston.

Sally was an attractive girl with red hair and bright, intelligent eyes. After the usual questions she said, 'Inspector, I would like to tell you that I think there's something very wrong about this house.'

'You mean you're afraid of something, Miss Finch?'

Sally nodded. 'Yes. The place isn't what it seems. And I'll bet you that awful old Mrs Nicoletis knows about it.'

'That's interesting. Can you be clearer?'

Sally shook her head. 'No. All I can tell you is that something unpleasant is going on here, Inspector. Other people feel it too. Akibombo does. He's frightened. I believe Elizabeth does, but she wouldn't say anything. And I think that Celia knew something about it.'

'Knew something about what?'

'There were things she said that last day. About clearing everything up. She had admitted *her* part in what was going on, but I think she knew *something*, about *someone*. That's the reason I think she was killed.'

'But if it was something as serious as that . . .'

Sally interrupted him. 'I think she had no idea how serious it was.'

'I see. Thank you . . . Now the last time you saw Celia was in the common room after dinner last night?'

'I saw her after that. When I went up to bed she was going out of the front door.'

'That's rather surprising.'

'I think she was going to meet someone.'

'Someone from outside. Or one of the students?'

'Well, I think that it was one of the students. Because if she wanted to speak to somebody privately, there was nowhere she could do it in the house.'

'Do you know when she returned?'

'No.'

'Thank you, Miss Finch.'

Last of all the Inspector talked to Elizabeth Johnston. 'Celia Austin said that it was not she who damaged your papers. Do you believe her?'

'I do not think Celia did it. No.'

'You don't know who did?'

'The obvious answer is Nigel Chapman. But it seems to me a little too obvious. Nigel is clever. He would not use his own ink.'

'And if not Nigel, who then?'

'That is more difficult. But I think Celia knew who it was.'

'Did she tell you so?'

'Not really; but yesterday evening before dinner she came to tell me that though she had stolen the things, she had not damaged my work. I said I believed her, then asked if she knew who had done so.'

'And what did she say?'

'She said –' Elizabeth paused a moment, 'she said, "I can't really be sure, because I don't see why . . . It might have been a mistake or an accident . . . I'm sure whoever did it would really like to admit it. And there are some things I don't understand, like the light bulbs the day the police came."'

'What's this about the police and light bulbs?'

'I don't know. All Celia said was, "*I* didn't take them out." And then she said, "I wondered if it had anything to do with the passport?" I said, "What passport?" And she said: "I think someone might have a forged passport."'

The Inspector was silent. Here at last a faint pattern seemed to be taking shape. A passport . . . 'What more did she say?'

'She just said, "Anyway I shall know more about it tomorrow."'

'*I shall know more about it tomorrow.* That's a very interesting remark.'

The Inspector was again silent as he considered.

Before coming to Hickory Road with Sergeant Cobb, he had looked up the records. Hostels which housed foreign students were carefully watched. Number 26 Hickory Road had a good record. There had only been one inquiry when there was a routine check of all hostels for a foreign student wanted for the murder of a woman near Cambridge. This had happened some time ago and could not possibly have any connection with the death of Celia Austin.

He looked up to see Elizabeth Johnston's dark intelligent eyes watching him and suddenly said, 'Have you ever had a feeling that something was *wrong* about this place?'

She looked surprised. 'In what way – wrong?'

'I don't really know. I'm thinking of something Miss Finch said to me.'

'Oh – Sally Finch! Americans are all the same, suspicious of everything!'

The Inspector's interest grew. So Elizabeth disliked Sally Finch. Why? Because Sally was an American? Or did Elizabeth dislike Americans just because Sally was an American?

He said, 'You understand, Miss Johnston, we just ask most people for facts. But when we meet someone with a high level of intelligence – ' He paused. Would she respond?

She did. 'What you want is the clarity of a trained mind.'

Inspector Sharpe nodded. 'That's why I would value your opinion.'

Elizabeth said, 'Don't listen to Sally Finch, Inspector. This is a good, well-run hostel. I am certain that you will find no illegal political activities here.'

Inspector Sharpe was surprised. 'It wasn't really political activities I was thinking about.'

'Oh – I see – ' She was a little confused. 'I was thinking of what Celia said about a passport. But I am sure that the reason for Celia's death was a private one.'

'I see. Well, thank you, Miss Johnston.'

Inspector Sharpe sat staring at the closed door, then turned to Sergeant Cobb. 'I'm coming back here tomorrow, Sergeant, with a search warrant. *There's something going on in this place.*'

Chapter 12

I

Hercule Poirot paused in the middle of a sentence that he was dictating and waved a hand. 'This letter is not important. If you please, Miss Lemon, get me your sister on the telephone.'

A few moments later he took the receiver from his secretary's hand. 'I trust, Mrs Hubbard, that I am not disturbing you?'

'Not at all. I'm so glad you've phoned, Monsieur Poirot.'

'There have been difficulties, yes?'

'That's a very nice way of saying it. Inspector Sharpe came with a search warrant today and I've got Mrs Nicoletis here shouting at me.'

'I am sorry,' Poirot said, 'it is just a little question I have to ask. You sent me a list of those things that had disappeared, but did you write that list in the order they were taken?'

'No, I'm sorry, I just wrote them down as I thought of them.'

'Would it be too difficult for you to remember and write what was the proper order?'

'Well, the rucksack, I believe, was the first, and the light bulbs and then the bracelet and the compact, no – the evening shoe. Anyway, I'll do the best I can.'

'Thank you, *Madame*.' Poirot hung up the phone. 'I am displeased with myself, Miss Lemon. I forgot to employ my usual principles of order and method. I should have made quite sure from the start, the exact sequence of these events.'

II

On arrival back at Hickory Road with a search warrant, Inspector Sharpe had demanded an interview with Mrs Nicoletis, who always came on Saturdays to do the accounts. He had explained what he was about to do.

'But it is an insult, that!' Mrs Nicoletis said. 'My students, they will all leave. I shall be ruined . . .'

'Madam, this is a murder case.'

'It is not murder – it is suicide.'

'So, I'll start here, in your sitting room.'

'Here, *no*! I refuse,' Mrs Nicoletis shouted. '*I* am above the law.'

'No one is above the law. So, please, stand aside.' He started with the desk. A large box of chocolates and a mass of papers were all he found. He moved from there to a cupboard. 'This is locked. Can I have the key, please?'

'Never!' shouted Mrs Nicoletis. 'You will have to tear my clothes off me before you get the key!'

'Get the tool, Cobb,' said Inspector Sharpe.

Mrs Nicoletis gave a cry of anger. Inspector Sharpe took no notice. The tool was brought. Two sharp cracks and the door was open and a large collection of empty brandy bottles poured out of the cupboard.

'Pig!' cried Mrs Nicoletis.

'Thank you, Madam,' said the Inspector. 'We've finished in here.' One mystery, the mystery of Mrs Nicoletis's moods, was now solved.

III

'Drink this,' said Mrs Hubbard, handing Mrs Nicoletis a cup of tea. 'And you'll soon feel better. There is nothing more to worry about now.'

'That is all very well for *you*. Me, I have to worry. It is not safe for me any longer.'

'Safe?' Mrs Hubbard looked at her, surprised.

'It was my private cupboard,' Mrs Nicoletis insisted. 'Nobody knew what was in my private cupboard. And now they *do* know. They may think – what will they think?'

'Who do you mean by *they*?'

Mrs Nicoletis shook her head. 'Thank goodness I do not sleep here.'

Mrs Hubbard said, 'Mrs Nicoletis, if you are afraid of something, wouldn't it be best to tell me what it is?'

Mrs Nicoletis gave her a quick look from her dark eyes. 'You have said yourself, there has been a murder in this house, so who may be next?'

'Then tell me if you have any reason to be so anxious . . .'

Mrs Nicoletis interrupted her. 'You are a spy – I always knew it. If lies are told about me I shall know who told them.'

'If you wish me to leave,' said Mrs Hubbard, 'you only have to say so.'

'No, you are not to leave. I will not allow it.'

'Oh, all right,' said Mrs Hubbard. 'But really, it's very difficult to know what you *do* want. Sometimes I don't think you know *yourself* what you want.'

Chapter 13

Hercule Poirot stepped from a taxi at 26 Hickory Road. The door was opened by Geronimo. 'Is Mrs Hubbard in?'

'I take you upstairs to her.'

'A little moment.' Poirot stopped him. 'Do you remember the day when certain electric light bulbs disappeared?'

'Yes, I remember.'

'Exactly what bulbs were taken?'

'The one in the hall and I think in the common room.'

'Do you remember the date?'

Geronimo thought. 'I think it was on the day when a policeman come, some time in February – '

'A policeman? What did a policeman come here for?'

'He come here to see Mrs Nicoletis about a man who murdered a woman somewhere else.'

'And that was the day the bulbs were missing?'

'Yes. Because I turn switch and nothing happen. And I look in drawer for more and I see bulbs have gone. So I use just candles.'

Poirot thought about this as he followed Geronimo up to Mrs Hubbard's room.

She was looking very tired and held out a piece of paper to him. 'I've done my best to write down these things in the proper order, but I'm not sure that it's completely accurate.'

'I am deeply grateful to you, *Madame*.' Poirot looked at the piece of paper. 'I see now that the rucksack is first. You had, I believe, a visit from the police here? And it was after that that you found the rucksack?'

'Yes. Len Bateson was going off on a hitch-hike and he couldn't find his rucksack anywhere, and everyone looked, and at last Geronimo found it behind the boiler, all cut up. So strange and pointless, Monsieur Poirot.'

'Yes, strange and pointless.' Poirot paused. 'How soon after this did the stealing begin?'

'I think . . . yes, Geneviève said she had missed her bracelet about a week after that. Between 20th and 25th February.'

'And after that the stealing went on?'

'Yes.'

'And this rucksack, was Len Bateson very angry about it?'

'Yes. But Len is that type of boy, Monsieur Poirot,' said Mrs Hubbard, smiling. 'He's also very generous, and kind.'

'What was it, this rucksack – something special?'

'Oh no, it was just ordinary.'

'Could you show me one like it?'

'Of course. Colin's got one. So has Nigel – in fact Len's got one again now because he had to go and buy another. They get them at the shop at the end of the road. It's much cheaper than any of the big stores.' Mrs Hubbard led him to Colin McNabb's room, opened the cupboard and picked up a rucksack.

'It would take some strength to cut that,' said Poirot.

'Oh yes, strength and – well – anger, you know.'

'I know, yes, it is not pleasant.'

'Then, when later that scarf of Valerie's was found, also cut to pieces, well, it did look – unbalanced.'

'Ah,' said Poirot. 'But I think there you are wrong, *Madame*. I do not think there is anything unbalanced about this business. I think it has purpose, and shall we say, method? You say that these rucksacks are bought at the shop at the end of the road?'

'Yes.'

Poirot thanked Mrs Hubbard, then left the house and walked down Hickory Road until he came to the shop. In the window was a lot of sports equipment. Poirot entered and said he would like to buy a rucksack for his nephew who was going hitch-hiking.

The man said, 'Ah, hitch-hiking. They all do it nowadays, all over Europe some of these young people go. Now, here is the usual one we sell. Good, strong, and really very cheap,' he said as he wrapped it up.

Poirot paid him and went out with his package. He had only gone a step or two when he felt a hand on his shoulder.

'Just the man I want to see,' said Inspector Sharpe. 'There's a place along here where you can get a cup of coffee, if you're not busy.'

The place was almost empty. The men carried their cups to a small table in a corner and Sharpe told Poirot the results of his interviews with the students. 'The only person we've got any evidence against is Chapman,' he said. 'And there we've got too much. Three lots of poison in his possession! But I doubt he would have been as honest about his activities if he was guilty.'

'And your hunt through the house – did you find anything?'

'Patricia Lane, in her drawer, had a handkerchief covered in green ink.'

'Green ink?' Poirot said. 'Patricia Lane! So it may have been she who spilled it over Elizabeth Johnston's papers and then wiped her hands afterwards. But surely . . .'

'Surely she wouldn't want her dear Nigel to be suspected,' Sharpe finished for him.

'But, of course, someone else might have put the handkerchief in her drawer. Anything else?'

'Well, it seems Leonard Bateson's father is in a mental hospital. Bateson's a nice fellow, but his temper is a bit, well, uncontrolled.'

Poirot nodded. Suddenly he remembered Celia Austin saying that it wasn't her who cut up the rucksack; that it was done with anger. How did she know it was done with anger? Had she seen Len Bateson attacking that rucksack?

'But we didn't find what we wanted. No forged passports.'

'You cannot really expect such a thing as a false passport to be left about for you to find, my good friend. Things will only make sense if we begin at the beginning.'

'What do you call the beginning, Poirot?'

'The rucksack,' said Poirot softly. 'All this began with a rucksack.'

Chapter 14

I

'I shall come in as usual on Monday,' said Mrs Nicoletis to Mrs Hubbard. 'I want new electric light bulbs put in the dark passages – stronger ones.'

'But you said especially that you wanted low-power bulbs – for economy.'

'That was last week,' said Mrs Nicoletis. '*Now* – it is different. Now I look over my shoulder – and I wonder who is following me.'

Mrs Hubbard said, 'Are you sure you ought to go home by yourself?'

'I shall be safer there than here, I can tell you!'

'But what is it you are afraid of? If I knew, perhaps I could – '

'I tell you nothing. It is not your business.'

'I'm sorry. I'm sure – '

'Now you are offended.' Mrs Nicoletis gave her a wide smile. 'But remember, I trust you, dear Mrs Hubbard. Good night.'

Mrs Nicoletis went out of the front door, down the steps to the gate and turned to the left. At the end of Hickory Road there were traffic lights on the corner, and a public house, *The Queen's Head*. Mrs Nicoletis walked in the middle of the path and occasionally looked over her shoulder, but there was no one there. When she reached *The Queen's Head*, after another quick look, she stepped inside.

Sipping a double brandy, she felt better, then turned violently as a voice behind her said, 'Why, Mrs Nick, I didn't know you came here?'

'Oh, it's you,' she said. 'I thought . . .'

'Who did you think it was? Some big bad man? What are you drinking? I'll get you another.'

'It is all the worry,' Mrs Nicoletis explained. 'These policemen searching my house. I do not like drinking, but I just thought a little brandy . . .'

'Nothing like brandy. Here you are.'

Mrs Nicoletis left *The Queen's Head* a short while later feeling positively happy. One brandy less, perhaps, would have been wise, but why shouldn't a lady have a quiet drink sometimes? And if they complained, then she would tell them that *she* knew a thing or two. So if she decided to talk . . . Mrs Nicoletis stepped sharply aside to avoid a postbox. Her head *did* feel a little strange. Perhaps if she just leant against the wall here for a little? If she closed her eyes for a moment or two . . .

II

Hercule Poirot was in his sitting room. Neatly arranged on the table were four rucksacks – the result of instructions given to his servant, George. Poirot took the rucksack he had bought the day before, and added it to the others. It did not seem any different from them, but it was very much cheaper.

He examined them all very carefully, inside and outside, turning them upside down, feeling the seams, the pockets, the handles. Then he picked up a small sharp knife and, turning the rucksack he had bought at Mr Hicks's shop inside out, he attacked the bottom of it. Between the inner lining and the bottom there was a heavy piece of cloth. Poirot looked at the rucksack with extreme interest.

Then he began to attack the other rucksacks. Finally, he sat back and took out the new list that Mrs Hubbard had given him. It was as follows:

Rucksack (Len Bateson's)
Electric light bulbs
Bracelet (Geneviève's)
Diamond ring (Patricia's)
Powder compact (Geneviève's)
Evening shoe (Sally's)
Lipstick (Elizabeth Johnston's)
Earrings (Valerie's)
Stethoscope (Len Bateson's)
Bath salts (?)
Scarf cut in pieces (Valerie's)
Trousers (Colin's)
Cookery book (?)
Boracic powder (Chandra Lal's)
Costume brooch (Sally's)
Ink spilled on Elizabeth's notes.
(This is the best I can do. L. Hubbard.)

Poirot looked at it for a long time, then said to himself, 'Yes . . . we have to eliminate the things that do not matter . . .'

He had an idea of who could help him. It was Sunday, so most of the students would be at home. He phoned 26 Hickory Road.

A short time later Geronimo opened the door and led the way upstairs into a good-sized room overlooking Hickory Road. The bed was decorated with a silk cover, and there was some attractive old furniture.

'Well, you have made this place very nice, Miss Hobhouse,' said Poirot. 'It has style.'

Valerie smiled. 'I've been here a long time, so I've got some of my own things.'

'You are not a student, are you, *Mademoiselle*?'

'Oh no. I'm one of the buyers for Sabrina Fair – it's a beauty salon. Actually I have a small share in the business. We also sell a few small things from Paris, and that's my department.'

'You go over fairly often to Paris?'

'About once a month, sometimes more. Please do sit down, Monsieur Poirot.'

Poirot sat in a high-backed chair. Valerie sat on the bed. She had a nervous, rather tired beauty and he wondered if her nervousness was the result of the recent inquiry, or whether it was a part of her usual manner.

'Inspector Sharpe has been asking questions of you?' he asked.

'Yes.'

'And you have told him all that you know?'

'Of course.'

'I wonder,' he said, 'if that is true.'

She gave him a humorous look. 'Since you did not hear my answers, you can't know anything about it.'

'Ah, it is just one of my little ideas. I have them, you know – the little ideas. They are here.' He touched his head.

But Valerie did not smile as he had expected. 'Why don't you get to the point, Monsieur Poirot? I really don't know what it is you want.'

'But certainly, Miss Hobhouse.' He took from his pocket a little package. 'You can guess, perhaps, what I have in here?'

'I'm not a fortune-teller, Monsieur Poirot.'

'I have here the ring that was stolen from Miss Patricia Lane.'

'Her mother's engagement ring? But why do *you* have it?'

'I asked her to lend it to me. I took it to a jeweller friend of mine and I asked him to report on the diamond. A large stone with some small stones on either side. You remember – *Mademoiselle*?'

'Not very well.'

'But it was in your soup plate.'

'That was how it was returned! I remember that. I nearly swallowed it.' Valerie gave a short laugh.

'Do you know what my friend said about the stone?'

'How could I?'

'He said that the stone was not a diamond. It was just a zircon.'

'Oh! Do you mean that – Patricia thought it was a diamond, but it was only a zircon or . . .'

Poirot was shaking his head. 'No, I do not mean that. Miss Lane is a young lady of good family, and I am certain that the Pappa of Miss Lane would not have given her Mamma anything but a valuable engagement ring. Therefore, it seems that the stone must have been changed for another stone later.'

'I suppose,' said Valerie, 'that Pat might have lost the stone out of it, couldn't afford another diamond, so had a zircon put in instead.'

'That is possible, but I do not think it is what happened.'

'Well, what *do* you think happened?'

'I think that the ring was taken by Mademoiselle Celia and that the diamond was removed and the zircon put there before the ring was returned.'

Valerie sat up very straight. 'You think that Celia stole that diamond?'

Poirot shook his head. 'No, I think *you* stole it, *Mademoiselle*.'

'Well, really! You have no evidence for saying that.'

'But, yes,' Poirot interrupted her. 'I have evidence. The ring was returned in a plate of soup. Now me, I dined here one evening, and the soup was served from a pot on the side table. Therefore, if anyone found a ring in their soup plate it could only have been placed there *either* by the person who was serving the soup (in this case Geronimo) or by the person whose soup plate it was. *You!* I think that *you* arranged the return of the ring in the soup in that way because it amused you. To hold up the ring! To pretend great surprise! I think you did not understand that you told the truth about yourself by so doing.'

'Is that all?' Valerie spoke coldly.

'Oh, no. You see, when Celia spoke of this ring she said, "I didn't know how valuable it was. As soon as I knew I returned it." Who told her how valuable the ring was? And then when she spoke of the cut scarf, Celia said something like, "Valerie didn't mind . . ." Why did you not mind? I formed the idea then that the plan of pretending to be a kleptomaniac, and so attracting the attention of Colin McNabb, had been thought out for Celia by *someone else*. *You* told her the ring was valuable; you took it from her and arranged its return. In the same way it was you who suggested that she cut a scarf of yours to pieces.'

Valerie gave a short laugh. 'You're quite right. It was all my idea.'

'May I ask you why?'

'Oh, there was Celia, so in love with Colin, who never looked at her. It all seemed so *silly*. So I spoke to her and explained the idea. She was a bit nervous, but rather excited at the same time. Then, of course, one of the first things the stupid girl does is to take Pat's ring – a really valuable piece of jewellery which might mean that the police would be called in. So I told her I would return it somehow, and that she must just take cheap things and perhaps do a little damage to something of mine which wouldn't get her into trouble.'

Poirot drew a deep breath. 'That was exactly what I thought. And now, we come to this business of Patricia's ring. *Before* returning it to her, what happened? You were short of money, was that it?'

Without looking at him she nodded. 'The trouble is, Monsieur Poirot, I'm a gambler. I belong to a little club in Mayfair and I've lost rather a lot recently. Then I thought, if this diamond was replaced with a white zircon, Pat would never know the difference! So I sold the diamond and replaced it with a zircon. There! Now you know it all. But honestly, I never meant Celia to be blamed for it.'

'No, no, I understand.' Poirot said. 'But you made a great mistake, *Mademoiselle*.'

'I know that,' said Valerie. Then she cried out, 'But what does that matter now? Tell the police if you like. Tell Pat. Tell the world! But how's it going to help us find out who killed Celia?'

Poirot stood up. 'One never knows what may help and what may not. But I suggest that you go to Miss Patricia Lane and tell her what you did.'

Valerie did not look happy. 'All right. And I'll tell her that when I can afford it, I'll buy her another diamond.'

The door opened suddenly and Mrs Hubbard came in. She was breathing fast and her expression made Valerie ask, 'What's the matter, Mum? What's happened?'

'It's Mrs Nicoletis.'

'Mrs Nick? What about her?'

'Oh, my dear. She's *dead*.'

'Dead?' Valerie's voice sounded rough. 'How? When?'

'She was found in the street last night – they took her to the police station. They thought she was – '

'Drunk? I suppose . . .'

'Yes – she *had* been drinking. But anyway – she died – '

'Poor old Mrs Nick,' said Valerie.

Poirot said gently, 'You were fond of her, *Mademoiselle*?'

'It's strange – but yes – I was . . . When I first came here, she wasn't nearly as – as difficult as she became later. She was funny, warm-hearted. She's changed a lot in the last year – '

Mrs Hubbard said, 'I do blame myself – letting her go off home alone last night – she was afraid of something.'

'Afraid?' Poirot and Valerie said it together.

Mrs Hubbard nodded. 'Yes. She kept saying she wasn't safe. I asked her to tell me what she was afraid of – and she refused. Now – I wonder – '

Valerie said, 'You don't think that she – that she, too was – ' She stopped, a look of fear in her eyes.

Poirot asked, 'What did they say was the cause of death?'

Mrs Hubbard said, 'They didn't say. There will be an inquest – on Tuesday – '

Chapter 15

In a quiet room at Scotland Yard, four men were sitting round a table.

The policemen were Superintendent Wilding of the Drugs division, Sergeant Bell, and Inspector Sharpe. The fourth man was Hercule Poirot. On the table was a rucksack.

'It's an interesting idea, Monsieur Poirot,' Superintendent Wilding said. 'Smuggling goes on all the time, of course. There's been a lot of heroin coming into this country in the last year and a half.'

'And what about other things, such as jewels?'

Sergeant Bell spoke. 'There's a lot of it going on, sir.'

Superintendent Wilding said, 'But Monsieur Poirot, what is it you're interested in, drugs or jewels?'

'Either. Anything of great value, but small in size. There is an opportunity, it seems to me, for what you might call a transport service, carrying things across the Channel. It could be a small, independent organization, unconnected with selling the things. And the profits might be high.'

'You're right about that!'

'You see,' said Poirot, 'the weakness of the smuggler is always that sooner or later you suspect a *person,* an air hostess, a sailing enthusiast, the woman who travels to France too often. But if the things are brought into this country *by a different person each time,* then it is very difficult to find the drugs or jewels.'

Wilding pointed at the rucksack. 'And that is how you think it is done?'

'Yes. Who is going to suspect a student, travelling about with just a rucksack on his back? And the great cleverness of the arrangement is that the carriers know nothing about what they are doing.'

'How exactly do you think it's managed?' Wilding asked.

'I think that it worked roughly like this: first, some rucksacks are made. They look ordinary, just like any other rucksack, but the lining at the bottom is different. As you see, it can easily be removed, and below is a space where jewels or drugs could be hidden.'

Wilding said, 'You could bring in drugs worth five or six thousand pounds each time, without anyone knowing.'

'Exactly,' said Hercule Poirot. 'The rucksacks are made, and put in probably more than one shop for sale. There is, of course, probably someone who is himself a student who is in charge of the whole thing. Students travel. At some point on the return journey, a rucksack that looks just the same is exchanged. The student returns to England, arrives back at the hostel, unpacks, and the empty rucksack is thrown into a corner. At this point the rucksack will again be exchanged.'

'And you think that's what happened at Hickory Road?'

Poirot nodded. 'That is my suspicion. Yes.'

'But what made you think of it, Monsieur Poirot?'

'A rucksack was cut to pieces. Why? It was hard work and someone must have been very anxious to do it. I got my clue when I found that the rucksack was destroyed at the time when a police officer called to see the person in charge of the hostel. The officer's call concerned another matter, but suppose you are someone involved in this smuggling, you immediately think that the police have come about the smuggling. And suppose that at that moment *there is in the house a rucksack* just brought back from abroad containing drugs. If there are drugs or jewels in the house, they can be hidden in bath salts. But even an empty rucksack, if it had held drugs, might show signs of heroin if it was examined. So, the rucksack must be destroyed.'

'It is an idea, as I said before,' said Superintendent Wilding.

'It also seems possible that some missing light bulbs may be connected with the rucksack. Perhaps someone was frightened that his face might be known to the police if they saw him in a bright light. So, he removed the bulb from the hall light and took away the new ones so that it could not be replaced.'

'But if what you say is true,' said Wilding, 'it must go beyond just Hickory Road?'

Poirot nodded. 'Oh yes. The organization must involve many students' hostels.'

'You have to find a connection between them,' said Wilding.

Inspector Sharpe spoke for the first time. 'There is such a connection, sir. Or there was. A woman who owned several hostels, Mrs Nicoletis.'

'Yes,' said Poirot. 'But I suspect she was not in charge of the whole operation.'

'Hm,' said Wilding. 'It would be interesting to know more about Mrs Nicoletis. Where is she?'

'She's dead, sir,' said Sharpe.

'Dead?' Wilding's eyes widened.

'Yes. We'll know for certain after she's been examined, but I think it could have been murder.'

'And Celia Austin, did she know something?'

'She knew something,' said Poirot, 'but I do not think she knew what it was she knew! So perhaps she mentioned the fact without understanding that it was important.'

'Have you any idea what she knew?'

'There has been mention of a passport. Did someone in the house have a false passport that allowed them to travel with another name? Did she see someone removing the false bottom from the rucksack? Did she perhaps see the person who removed the light bulbs? Guesses! Guesses! Guesses! One must *know* more!'

'Well,' said Sharpe, 'we can start by investigating Mrs Nicoletis's involvement. But you say she was not in charge of the organization. Have you any idea, Monsieur Poirot, who that might be?'

'I could make a guess – I might be wrong. Yes – I *might* be wrong!'

Chapter 16

I

'Please, Sally, may I ask you a question?'

Sally and Akibombo were having lunch together in a restaurant in Regent's Park.

'All this morning,' said Akibombo sadly, 'I have been very upset. I cannot answer my professor's questions at all. He is not pleased with me. But I find it very hard to think except of what goes on at Hickory Road.'

'I understand,' said Sally. 'I feel the same.'

'So that is why I am asking you please to tell me certain things. This boracic, it is an acid, they say? Something very strong?'

'No. It's harmless.'

'You mean, you could put it in your *eyes*?'

'That's right. That's what people use it for.'

'Ah, that explains that then. Mr Chandra Lal, he has little white bottle with white powder, and he puts powder in hot water and washes his eyes with it. He keeps it in bathroom and then it was not there one day and he was very angry. That would be boracic?'

'What *is* all this about boracic?'

'I'll tell you later. I need to think some more about it.'

'Well, don't go around telling everyone,' said Sally. 'I don't want yours to be the next dead body, Akibombo.'

II

'Valerie, do you think you could give me some advice?' said Jean. 'It's about doing the right thing.'

'Then I'm the last person you should ask. I never do the right thing – well not often.'

'Oh, Valerie, don't say things like that! But suppose you know something, something about someone, should you should tell the police?'

'What a stupid question! You can't answer something like that in general terms. What is it you want to tell, or don't want to tell?'

'It's about a passport.'

'A passport?' Valerie sat up. 'Whose passport?'

'Nigel's. He's got a false passport.'

'I don't believe it.'

'But he has. And, Valerie, suppose Celia found out about it and he killed her?'

'Sounds very unlikely. But how did you see Nigel's passport?'

'Well, I was looking for something in my case, and by mistake I must have looked in Nigel's case. They were both in the common room.'

Valerie laughed rather unkindly. 'What were you hoping to find?'

'Nothing! I just wasn't thinking properly, so I opened the case and I was just sorting through it . . .'

'Jean, that's nonsense. Nigel's case is much bigger than yours and it's a different colour. So, all right, you found a chance to look through Nigel's things and you did.'

Jean stood up. 'If you're going to be unpleasant, I shall . . .'

'Oh, sit down!' said Valerie. 'I'm getting interested now.'

'Well, there was this passport. And it had a name on it. Stanford or Stanley, and I thought, how strange that Nigel has somebody else's passport. I opened it and the photograph inside was Nigel!'

Valerie laughed. 'Bad luck, Jean. There's a simple explanation. Pat told me that Nigel was left some money on the condition that he changed his name. So that's all it is. His original name *was* Stanfield or Stanley, or something like that.'

'Oh!' Jean looked very disappointed.

'Better luck next time,' said Valerie.

'I don't know what you mean.'

'You would like to get Nigel in trouble with the police.'

'You may not believe me, Valerie, but all I wanted to do was my duty,' Jean said, and left the room.

III

'Nigel, I've got something I must tell you.'

'What is it, Pat?' Nigel was looking urgently inside his chest of drawers. 'What did I do with my notes?'

'Oh, Nigel, you must listen! I've got to tell the truth about something.'

'Not murder, I hope?' Nigel laughed. 'Hickory, dickory, dock, the mouse ran up the clock. The police said "Boo", I wonder who, will eventually stand in the dock?'

'No, of course not! But one day when I had mended your socks and was putting them away in your drawer . . .'

'Yes?'

'And the bottle of morphia was there. The one you told me about, Nigel, it was there in your drawer where *anybody* could have found it.'

'Why? Nobody else looks amongst my socks except you.'

'Well, I thought it was wrong, so I took the bottle out of the drawer and I emptied the poison out of it, and I replaced it with some bicarbonate of soda.'

'You mean that when I told Len and Colin that it was morphine, it was just bicarbonate of soda? But that might make the bet no good!'

'Nigel, it was really *dangerous* keeping it there.'

'So what did you do with the morphine?'

'I put it in the bicarbonate of soda bottle, and I hid it at the back of my handkerchief drawer.'

Nigel shook his head. 'Really, Pat, do you really have a brain? What was the point?'

'I felt it was safer there. I have a room of my own, and you share yours. I wasn't going to tell you about it, ever, but I must now. Because, you see, it's *gone*.'

'Do you mean . . . ?' Nigel looked shocked. 'There's a bottle with "Soda Bic" written on it, containing morphine, in this place somewhere, and at any time someone might take a spoonful of it if they've got a stomach pain? Why didn't you throw the drug away if you were so upset about it?'

'Because I thought it was valuable and ought to go back to the hospital. As soon as you had won your bet, I meant to ask Celia to put it back.'

'So when did it disappear?'

'I don't know. I looked for it the day before Celia died and couldn't find it.'

'It was gone the day *before* she died?'

'I suppose,' said Patricia, her face white, 'that I've been very stupid. Nigel, do you think I should tell the police?'

'I suppose so, yes. And it's going to be all my fault!'

'Oh, no, Nigel dear, it's me. I – '

'I was the one who stole it. It all seemed to be very amusing at the time, but now – Look, Pat, you've probably just forgotten where you put it.' Nigel stood up. 'Let's go along to your room and look.'

IV

'Nigel, those are my *underclothes.*'

'Really, Pat, you can't go all shy now. Down among the panties is just where you would hide a bottle, now, isn't it?'

'Yes, but I'm sure I – '

There was a slight knock on the door and Sally Finch entered. Her eyes widened. Pat, with a handful of Nigel's socks, was sitting on the bed, and Nigel was digging into a pile of clothes like an excited dog, while panties lay all around him.

'For goodness sake,' said Sally, 'what's going on?'

'Looking for bicarbonate,' said Nigel.

'Bicarbonate? Why?'

'I've got a pain,' he said, smiling. 'In my stomach.'

'I've got some, I believe.'

'No good, Sally, it's got to be Pat's. Hers is the only type that will help my particular problem.'

'You're mad,' said Sally.

'*You* haven't seen my bicarbonate, have you, Sally?' Pat asked.

'No.' Sally paused. 'But somebody here – no, I can't remember – Have you got a stamp, Pat? I want to send a letter and I haven't got any.'

'In the drawer there.'

Sally opened the drawer, found a book of stamps, took one, and put some money on the desk. 'Thanks. Shall I post this letter of yours at the same time?'

'Yes – no, I think I'll wait.'

When Sally had left the room, Pat dropped the socks and twisted her fingers nervously together. 'Nigel? There's something else I've got to tell you. I'm afraid you'll be angry.'

'I'm past being angry. I'm just frightened. If Celia was poisoned with the morphine that I stole, I shall probably go to prison.'

'It's nothing to do with that. It's about your father.'

'What?' Nigel turned, a shocked expression on his face.

'You do know he's very ill, don't you?'

'I don't care how ill he is.'

'It said so on the radio last night. "Sir Arthur Stanley, the chemist, is in a very bad condition."'

'So nice to be famous. All the world hears when you're ill.'

'Nigel, if he's dying, you should go to see him.'

'No, I certainly will not! He may be dying, but he's still the same person!'

'You mustn't be like that, Nigel. So unforgiving.'

'Listen, Pat – I told you once, he killed my mother.'

'I know you said so, and I know you loved her very much. But, Nigel, lots of husbands are unkind and it makes their wives unhappy. But to say your father killed your mother isn't really true.'

'You know so much about it, don't you?'

'I know that some day you'll be sorry that you didn't make peace with your father before he died. That's why – ' Pat paused. 'That's why I've written to your father – telling him – '

'You've written to him? Is that the letter Sally wanted to post?' Nigel walked over to the desk. He picked the letter up, tore it into small pieces and threw it into the waste paper basket. 'That's that!'

'Really, Nigel, you can tear the letter up, but you can't stop me writing another.'

'You're so stupid. Did you not understand that when I said my father killed my mother, I was stating just a plain *fact.* My mother died from taking too much of her sleeping medicine. They said at the inquest that she took it by mistake. *But she didn't take it by mistake.* It was given to her, deliberately, by my father. He wanted to marry another woman, and my mother wouldn't give him a divorce. It was plain murder. What would you have done in my place? Told the police? My mother wouldn't have wanted that . . . So I did the only thing I could do – told him I knew – and left home – for ever. I even changed my name.'

'Nigel – I'm sorry . . . I never dreamed . . .'

'Well, you know now . . . about the respected Arthur Stanley. But his other woman didn't marry him after all. I think she guessed what he had done – '

'Nigel dear, how awful . . .'

'All right. We won't talk of it again. Let's get back to this bicarbonate business. Now think back carefully to exactly what you did with the stuff. *Think,* Pat.'

Chapter 17

I

Sitting in a room at the police station, Nigel looked nervously into the eyes of Inspector Sharpe.

'You understand, Mr Chapman, that what you have just told us is very serious?' said the Inspector.

'Of course I understand. I wouldn't have come here to tell you about it unless I had felt it was important.'

'And you say Miss Lane can't remember exactly when she last saw this bicarbonate bottle containing morphine?'

'No, but she's trying to make some sense of it now.'

'We had better go round to Hickory Road immediately.'

As the Inspector spoke the telephone rang, and the constable who had been taking notes of Nigel's story answered. 'It's Miss Lane,' he said. 'Wanting to speak to Mr Chapman.'

Nigel leaned across the table and took the receiver. 'Pat? Nigel here.'

The girl's voice sounded breathless. 'Nigel. *I think I know!* I mean, who must have taken – you know – from my handkerchief drawer – you see, there's only one person who – ' The voice broke off.

'Pat. Are you still there? Who was it?'

'I can't tell you now. Later. You'll be coming round?'

The receiver was near enough for the Inspector to hear the voice clearly, and he nodded at Nigel.

'We're coming round right now,' said Nigel.

'Oh! Good. I'll be in my room.'

'Goodbye, Pat.'

Hardly a word was spoken during the short ride to Hickory Road. Nigel opened the front door and led the way upstairs to

Pat's room. He knocked and entered. 'Hello, Pat. Here we – ' He stopped.

Over Nigel's shoulder, Sharpe could see Patricia Lane lying on the floor. He pushed Nigel gently aside, then went across to the girl. He raised her head, felt for the pulse, then let the head rest back again.

'No?' said Nigel, his voice high and unnatural. 'No. No. *No.*'

'Yes, Mr Chapman, she's dead.' The Inspector stood up.

'No, *no*. Not Pat! Dear stupid Pat. How – '

'With this.' It was a simple weapon. A stone paperweight inside a sock. 'Hit on the back of the head. If it's any help to you, I don't think she knew what happened to her.'

Nigel sat down on the bed. 'That's one of *my* socks . . . She was going to mend it . . .' He began to cry like a child.

'Do you recognize the paperweight, Mr Chapman?' Sharpe rolled back the sock.

Nigel, still crying, looked. 'Pat always had it on her desk, a lion.' Suddenly he sat up straight, throwing back his untidy fair hair. 'I'll kill whoever did this! I'll kill him!'

'Gently, Mr Chapman.' Speaking kindly, Inspector Sharpe got him out of the room. Then he went back and leant over the dead girl. Very carefully he removed something from between her fingers.

II

Geronimo looked with frightened eyes at the Inspector. 'I see nothing. I hear nothing. I am with Maria in kitchen.'

'But you can see from the kitchen window who goes in and out, can't you?' Sharpe said. 'Who was in the house from six o'clock until six thirty-five when we arrived?'

'Everybody except Mr Nigel and Mrs Hubbard and Miss Hobhouse.'

'When did they go out?'

'Mrs Hubbard – she go out before tea-time, she has not come back yet. Mr Nigel goes out about half an hour ago, just before six – look very upset. He come back with you just now. Miss Valerie, she goes out just at six o'clock, dressed for party. She still out.'

Sharpe looked down at his notebook. The time of Patricia's call was written there. Eight minutes past six, exactly. 'Everybody else was here? Nobody came back during that time?'

'Only Miss Sally. She went down to postbox with letter and come back in.'

'Do you know what time she came in?'

Geronimo thought. 'She came back while the news was on the radio.'

'*After* six, then?'

'Yes, sir.'

III

In her room, Mrs Hubbard, still in her outdoor clothes, sat on the sofa.

'I think she telephoned from in here,' said Sharpe. 'Nobody saw or heard the hall telephone being used. You were out, Mrs Hubbard, but I don't suppose you lock your door?'

Mrs Hubbard shook her head.

'So Patricia Lane came in here to telephone, excited with what she had remembered. Then, while she was talking, somebody opened the door. Patricia paused and then ended the conversation. Was that because the person who had come in was the person whose name she was just about to say? And then that person went back to Patricia's room with her and perhaps Patricia asked her about taking the bicarbonate.'

Mrs Hubbard said sharply, 'Why do you say *"her"*?'

'Just this. Somebody went into Patricia's room with her – someone with whom she felt comfortable. That points to another girl. And if the conversation earlier between Nigel and Pat was heard, it was probably a girl who heard it. Which girls have the rooms on either side of Patricia's?'

'Geneviève's is on the far side – but that's a thick original wall. Elizabeth Johnston's is on the side nearer the stairs. That's only a thin wall.'

'But I've been told that she was already in the common room when Sally Finch went out to post her letter. She did go upstairs again to get a book. But nobody can say *when*.'

'It might have been any of them,' said Mrs Hubbard.

'As far as their statements go, yes – but we've got a little extra evidence.' Sharpe took a small paper bag out of his pocket.

'What's that?'

'Two hairs – I took them from between Patricia Lane's fingers.'

'You mean that – '

There was a knock on the door. 'Come in,' said the Inspector.

The door opened. 'Please,' Mr Akibombo said, 'I have a statement to make. A very important statement about this murder.'

Chapter 18

Mr Akibombo was offered a chair. 'Thank you. You see, sometimes I have a stomach ache. Sometimes I take a small pill, and sometimes stomach powder. After that,' Akibombo smiled, 'I feel much better.'

Mrs Hubbard said, 'We understand all about *that.* Now get on to the next part.'

'Yes. Well, as I say, this happens to me early last week. It was after supper in the common room and only Elizabeth was there and I say to her, "Have you bicarbonate, I have finished mine." And she says, "No. But, I saw some in Pat's drawer when I was putting back a handkerchief I borrowed from her. I will get it for you." So she goes upstairs and comes back with a bottle, almost empty. I thank her and I put a teaspoon of it in water and drink it.'

'A *teaspoon*? A teaspoon! The Inspector looked at him. 'You swallowed a teaspoon of *morphia*?'

'But I think it is bicarbonate. And then, afterwards, I was ill, but really ill.'

'I can't make out why you're not dead!'

Mr Akibombo continued. 'So then, next day, when I am better, I take the bottle and the tiny bit of powder that is left in it to a chemist and I say, please tell me what is this?'

'Yes?'

'And he says come back later, and then he says, "No wonder! This is not the bicarbonate. It is the boracic. You can put it in the eyes, yes, but if you swallow a teaspoonful it makes you ill."'

'Boracic? But how did boracic get into that bottle? What happened to the morphia?' Inspector Sharpe shook his head.

'I have been thinking,' said Akibombo, 'of Miss Celia and how she died and that someone, after she was dead, must have come into her room and left there the empty morphia bottle and the little piece of paper that say she killed herself.'

Akibombo paused and the Inspector nodded.

'And I think if it is one of the girls it will be easy, but if a man, not so easy. So I think, and I say, suppose it is someone in our house, but in the next room to Miss Celia's? Outside his window is a balcony and outside hers is a balcony too. So if he is big and strong he could jump across.'

'The room next to Celia's in the other house,' said Mrs Hubbard, 'Well, that's Nigel's and – and . . .'

'Len Bateson's.' The Inspector's finger touched the folded paper in his hand.

'Mr Chandra Lal was very angry when his boracic was not there and later, when I ask, he says he has been told that it was taken by Len Bateson . . .'

'The morphia was taken from Nigel's drawer and boracic was exchanged for it. Then Patricia Lane came along and exchanged soda bicarbonate for what she thought was morphia, but which was really boracic powder . . . Yes . . . I see . . .'

'I have helped you, yes?' Mr Akibombo asked politely.

'Yes, thank you. Don't – er – repeat any of this.'

'No, sir. I will be most careful.' Mr Akibombo left the room.

'Len Bateson,' said Mrs Hubbard. 'Oh! *No.* He's always seemed so *nice.*'

'That's been said about a lot of criminals,' said Sharpe. Gently he opened his little paper bag. In it were two red curly hairs . . .

'Oh dear,' said Mrs Hubbard.

Chapter 19

I

'But it is beautiful, my friend,' said Hercule Poirot. 'So clear – so beautifully clear. Everything fits in its correct place.'

'Even these?' Inspector Sharpe showed Poirot the two red hairs.

'Ah – yes, the one deliberate mistake.' The two men looked at each other. 'For the other investigation, my friend, it is all fixed?'

'Yes, for tomorrow.'

'You go yourself?'

'No. I plan to appear at 26 Hickory Road. Cobb will be in charge.'

'We will wish him good luck,' said Hercule Poirot

II

Sergeant Cobb marched boldly into the pink interior of Sabrina Fair, Detective Constable McCrae behind him. A beautiful creature moved towards them, her feet hardly seeming to touch the floor.

Sergeant Cobb said, 'Good morning, Madam,' and explained why he was there. The beautiful creature backed away and another beautiful, but much older creature with smooth hair and steel-grey eyes appeared.

'This is most unusual,' she said. 'Please come this way.' She led him through the salon into a room with a big desk, and several hard-backed chairs. 'I am Mrs Lucas, the owner of this place. My partner, Miss Hobhouse, is not here today.'

'No, Madam,' said Sergeant Cobb, who already knew that.

'This is her private office, and your search warrant seems to be most unnecessary,' said Mrs Lucas.

He waited politely until she left them alone. A quarter of an hour later, a safe and the drawers of the desk had been searched, but they had found nothing.

'Looks like we got it wrong,' said McCrae.

'We're only just beginning,' said Cobb. He took the drawers one after the other and turned them upside down. 'Here we are!' Fastened with tape underneath the bottom drawer were six small dark-blue books with gold lettering. 'Passports.'

McCrae watched as Cobb opened the passports and compared the photographs. 'You really wouldn't think it was the same woman, would you?'

The passports were those of Mrs da Silva, Miss Irene French, Mrs Olga Köhn, Miss Nina Le Mesurier, Mrs Gladys Thomas, and Miss Moira O'Neele. The photos were all of a dark young woman between the ages of twenty-five and forty.

'It's the different hairstyle that does it,' said Cobb. 'I expect she's got bank accounts in all these different names.'

'Bit complicated, that?'

'It has to be complicated. It's not so difficult to make money by smuggling – but it's very difficult to account for money when you've got it! I bet this little gambling club in Mayfair was started by the lady for just that reason. Winning money by gambling is about the only thing a tax inspector can't check. And then, one day, she must have left one of these false passports lying about at Hickory Road and poor little Celia saw it.'

Chapter 20

'It was a clever idea of Miss Hobhouse's,' said Inspector Sharpe, moving the passports from one hand to the other like a pack of cards. 'We've had a busy time racing round the banks. And we've got Monsieur Poirot here to thank for working it out. It was clever of her, too, to suggest that stealing trick to poor little Miss Austin. You saw it was a trick almost at once, didn't you, Monsieur Poirot?'

Poirot smiled. 'She could not let pass the chance of possessing that fine diamond in Patricia Lane's ring.'

'But murder!' said Mrs Hubbard. 'I can't really believe it, even now.'

'We aren't able to charge her with the murder yet,' said Sharpe. 'She could certainly have poisoned Mrs Nicoletis – but she definitely did not kill Patricia Lane. The chemist at the corner of the road says she came in at five minutes past six and bought face powder and aspirin and used the telephone. She left his shop at quarter-past six.'

Poirot sat up in his chair. 'But that is perfect! It is just what we want!'

'What do you mean?'

'I mean that she telephoned from the chemist's shop.'

Inspector Sharpe looked at him. 'Now, Monsieur Poirot, let's not forget the facts. At eight minutes past six, Patricia Lane is alive and telephoning to the police station from this room. You agree?'

'I do not think she was telephoning from this room.'

'Well then, from downstairs.'

'Not from downstairs either.'

Inspector Sharpe shook his head. 'You do agree that a call *was* received at the police station?'

'Certainly. A call was received by you. A call that came from the public call-box at the chemist's.'

Inspector Sharpe's mouth dropped open. 'You mean that *Valerie Hobhouse* made that call? That she pretended to speak as Patricia Lane, and that Patricia Lane was *already dead*.'

'That is what I mean, yes.'

The Inspector was silent for a moment, then his hand came down with a crash on the table. 'I don't believe it. The voice – I heard it myself – '

'You heard it, yes. A girl's voice. But you didn't know Patricia Lane's voice well enough to say that it *was* her voice.'

'*I* didn't, perhaps. But Nigel Chapman would have known if it wasn't Pat's voice.'

'Yes,' said Poirot. '*Nigel Chapman would have known.* Nigel Chapman knew very well that it *wasn't* Patricia. Who would know better than he, as he had killed her only a short while before.'

It was a moment or two before the Inspector spoke. 'Nigel Chapman? But when we found her dead he cried like a child.'

'I expect he did,' said Poirot. 'I think he cared about that girl as much as he could care for anybody – but that wouldn't save her – not if she was a threat to his interests. All along, Nigel Chapman has been the most likely murderer. Who had morphia in his possession? Nigel Chapman. Who had the sharp intelligence to plan and the nerve to commit murder? Nigel Chapman. Who cares nothing for anyone but himself? Nigel Chapman. He even wanted to draw attention to himself – using the green ink, and even by the silly deliberate mistake of putting Len Bateson's hairs in Patricia's fingers. He didn't care that as Patricia was hit from behind, she could not possibly have pulled her attacker's hair. They are like that, these murderers, excited by their love of their own cleverness and charm – for he *has* charm, this Nigel – all the charm of a spoiled child who has never grown up, who never will grow up – who sees only one thing, himself, and what he wants!'

'But why, Monsieur Poirot? Why murder? Celia Austin, perhaps, but why Patricia Lane?'

'That,' said Poirot, 'we have got to find out.'

Chapter 21

'I haven't seen you for a long time,' said old Mr Endicott to Hercule Poirot. 'It's very nice of you to call.'

'Not really,' said Hercule Poirot. 'I want something.'

'Well, as you know, I am very grateful to you. You cleared up that unpleasant Abernethie business for me.' The old lawyer smiled.

'Sir Arthur Stanley was a good friend, was he not?'

'Yes. And we've looked after his legal work since he was young.'

'His death was mentioned on the six o'clock news yesterday, I believe.'

'Yes. The funeral's on Friday.'

'Lady Stanley died some years ago?'

'Two and a half years ago.' He looked sharply at Poirot.

'How did she die?'

'Too much of a sleeping drug. The inquest found that she took it accidentally.'

'Did she?'

Mr Endicott was silent for a moment. 'It seems so. There was no suggestion of suicide.'

'And no suggestion of – anything else?'

Again he looked sharply at Poirot. 'Her husband said that she did sometimes get confused after taking the drug and ask for more.'

'Was he lying?'

'Really, Poirot, why do you think that I could possibly know?'

Poirot smiled. 'I think, my friend, that you know very well. But I will not embarrass you by asking you that. Instead I will ask you for an opinion. Was Arthur Stanley the type of man who would kill his wife if he wanted to marry another woman?'

Mr Endicott was shocked. 'Certainly not! And there was no other woman. Stanley loved his wife.'

'Yes,' said Poirot. 'I thought so. And now I will tell you the purpose of my call. Arthur Stanley had a son. The son quarrelled with his father at the time of his mother's death, and then left home. He even changed his name.'

'That I did not know.'

'So did Arthur Stanley leave a letter with you, a letter to be opened under certain conditions or after his death?'

'Poirot, how can you possibly know the things you do?'

'I am right then? I think there were two choices in the letter. It was either to be destroyed – or you were to perform a certain action.'

'This matter is private. Even from you, Poirot – ' Mr Endicott shook his head.

'And if I show you good cause why you should speak?'

'How can you possibly know anything at all about this matter?'

Poirot took a deep breath. 'It is in my mind that your instructions are these. If Sir Arthur dies, you are to find his son Nigel, and discover if he is involved in any criminal activity.'

This time Mr Endicott gave a sharp sound of surprise. 'Well, as you seem to know all about it, I'll tell you anything you want to know. You must have met young Nigel in the course of your professional activities. What's he done now?'

'I think the story goes like this. After he had left home, he changed his name. He then met some people who were involved in smuggling – drugs and jewels. I think it was his idea to use innocent students to carry things. The whole operation was organized by two people, Nigel Chapman, as he now called himself, and a young woman called Valerie Hobhouse. Everything went well until one day a police officer came to a students' hostel to ask questions about a murder near Cambridge. But Nigel thought the police were after *him*. He removed certain electric bulbs so that the light would be faint, and he also took a certain rucksack outside, cut it to pieces and threw it behind the boiler. He was afraid some remains of drugs might be found in its false bottom. His fear was unnecessary, but one of the girls in the hostel had happened to look out of her window and had seen him destroying the rucksack. That did not immediately mean she had to die. Instead, she was persuaded to commit certain stupid actions which would put her in a difficult position. But they pushed that idea too far. I was called in.

'I advised going to the police. The girl was frightened and admitted what she had done. But *only* the things she had done. And she went, I think, to Nigel, and urged him to admit to the rucksack business and to spilling ink over a fellow student's work. Neither Nigel nor Valerie could consider calling attention to the rucksack – their whole plan would be ruined. Celia, the young girl, she knew too much. The next evening she went out to meet Nigel somewhere. He gave her some coffee and in it was morphia. She died in her sleep with everything arranged to look like suicide.'

An expression of deep upset crossed Mr Endicott's face.

'But that was not the end,' said Poirot. 'The woman who owned the hostels died soon after and then, finally, there came the last, most cruel and heartless crime. Patricia Lane, a girl who loved Nigel, told him that he should go to see his father before he died. He told her some lies about his family, and destroyed her letter to his father, but he knew that she might write a second letter. I think, my friend, that you can tell me why that would have been such a deadly thing to happen.'

Mr Endicott stood up, went across to a safe, unlocked it, and came back with a long envelope in his hand. He took out two letters and laid them before Poirot.

Dear Endicott,

You will open this after I am dead. I wish you to find my son Nigel and discover if he has been guilty of any criminal actions.

Nigel has twice been guilty of forging my name to a cheque. On each occasion I said the signature was mine, but warned him that I would not do so again. On the third occasion it was his mother's name he forged. He asked her to keep silent. She refused. It was then that he put an extra amount of her sleeping mixture into her glass. Before she fell asleep, however, she had told me about the cheque. When, the next morning, she was found dead, I knew who had done it.

I told Nigel that I intended to go to the police. He was very upset and kept asking me not to. What would you have done, Endicott? I know my son is one of those dangerous people who have no sense of pity. I had no reason to save him. But it was the thought of my wife that decided me. Would she wish me to bring our son to justice? I thought that I knew the answer – she would have wanted him saved.

But I firmly believe that once a killer, always a killer. There might be, in the future, other victims. I made a deal with my son, and whether I did right or wrong, I do not know. He was to write out a confession of his crime which I would keep. He was to leave my house and never return. I would give him a second chance. Money belonging to his mother would come to him. He had had a good education. He had every chance of making a better life for himself.

But – if he committed any criminal activity at all, the confession he had left with me would go to the police. I also made myself safe because my own death would not prevent that happening.

You are my oldest friend. Find Nigel. If his record is clean, destroy both these letters. If not – then justice must be done.

Your loving friend,

Arthur Stanley

'Ah!' Poirot breathed out and unfolded the other piece of paper.

I hereby confess that I murdered my mother by giving her an extra amount of her sleeping medicine on November 18th.

Nigel Stanley

Chapter 22

'You understand your position, Miss Hobhouse. I have already warned you – '

Valerie Hobhouse interrupted Sharpe. 'That what I say will be used in evidence. I'm prepared for that. You've got me on the smuggling charge. But this other information means that I'll be charged in connection with a murder.'

'Making a statement may help you, but I can't promise that.'

'I don't really care. I never intended murder or wanted it. What I do want is a clear case against Nigel . . . Celia knew too much, but I could have managed that. Nigel didn't give me time. He killed her and then told me what he had done. The same thing happened with Mrs Nick. He had found out that she drank, that she couldn't be trusted – so he met her somewhere on her way home, and poisoned her drink. Then there was Pat. He came up to my room and told me what had happened. He told me what I had to do – so that both he and I would have an alibi. I was caught by then . . . but now I only care about one thing – to make sure that Nigel gets punished.'

'I'm not sure that I understand . . .' began Sharpe.

'You don't need to understand. I've got my reasons.'

Hercule Poirot spoke very gently. 'Mrs Nicoletis, she was – your mother, was she not?'

'Yes,' said Valerie Hobhouse. 'She was my mother . . .'

Chapter 23

I

'I do not understand.' Mr Akibombo looked from one red head to the other.

'Do you think,' asked Sally Finch, 'that Nigel meant *me* to be suspected, or you?'

'Either, I expect,' replied Len Bateson. 'I believe he took the hairs from *my* brush.'

'Was it then Mr Nigel who jumped the balcony?' asked Mr Akibombo.

'Nigel can jump like a cat,' said Len. 'I couldn't have jumped across that space. I'm much too heavy.'

'I want to apologize for my suspicions,' said Akibombo.

'That's all right,' said Len.

'In fact, you helped a lot,' said Sally. 'All your thinking – about the boracic.'

He smiled. 'If you meet my professor at the University party tonight will you tell him, please, that I have done some good thinking?'

'I'll tell him,' said Sally.

Len Bateson was looking unhappy. 'In a week's time you'll be back in America.'

'I shall come back. Or you might come and study over there.'

'What's the use?'

'Akibombo,' said Sally, 'would you like, one day, to be best man at a wedding?'

'What do you mean, best man?'

'The <u>bridegroom</u>, for example Len here, gives you a ring to keep for him, and he and you go to church very smartly dressed, and at the right moment, he asks you for the ring and you give it to him, and he puts it on my finger, and then the wedding march is played and everybody cries. And there we are.'

'You mean that you and Mr Len are to be married?'

'That's the idea.'

'*Sally!*'

'Unless, of course, Len doesn't like the idea.'

'*Sally!* If you only knew how happy you've made me.'

'I do have just a tiny suspicion.'

II

Hercule Poirot signed the last of the letters that Miss Lemon had laid before him.

'Very good,' he said. 'Not a single mistake.'

'I don't often make mistakes, I hope,' Miss Lemon said.

'Not often. But it has happened. How is your sister, by the way?'

'She is thinking of going on a cruise, Monsieur Poirot.'

'Ah.' Hercule Poirot wondered if – possibly – on a cruise – ? Not that he himself would ever go on one – not for any reason . . .

The clock behind him struck one.

'The clock struck one,
The mouse ran down,
Hickory, dickory, dock,' said Hercule Poirot.

'What was that, Monsieur Poirot?'

'Nothing,' said Hercule Poirot.

Character list

Monsieur Hercule Poirot: the famous Belgian detective

Miss Lemon: Hercule Poirot's secretary

Mrs Hubbard (Ma or Mum): Miss Lemon's sister who looks after a student hostel at 26 Hickory Road

Miss Patricia Lane: a student studying History

Miss Valerie Hobhouse: a young woman who lives at the hostel, but works at a beauty salon

Leonard Bateson: a student studying Medicine

Colin McNabb: a student studying Psychology

Sally Finch: an American student, studying Science

Mrs Nicoletis (Mrs Nick): the half-Greek owner of 26 Hickory Road and other hostels

Nigel Chapman: a student studying Italian

Elizabeth Johnston: a Jamaican student, studying Law

Celia Austin: works at the pharmacy at St Catherine's Hospital

Geneviève Maricaud: a French student studying English

Jean Tomlinson: a physiotherapist at St Catherine's Hospital

Mr Akibombo: a West African student at London University

Chandra Lal: an Indian student at the hostel

Geronimo: the Italian manservant at 26 Hickory Road, whose wife Maria is the cook

Inspector Sharpe: a police officer from Scotland Yard dealing with the murder case

Sergeant Cobb: a Scotland Yard police officer working on the case

Superintendent Wilding: a senior police officer in the Drugs Division

Sergeant Bell: a police officer working on the case

Detective Constable McCrae: a police officer working on the case

Mrs Lucas: the owner of a beauty salon

Mr Endicott: Sir Arthur Stanley's lawyer

Sir Arthur Stanley: the father of one of the students

Cultural notes

Communists

Nigel and Colin are both accused of being communists and this is not unusual during the 1950s when Agatha Christie wrote the novel. There was a lot of anti-communist feeling in Britain as a result of the Cold War. The Cold War, which lasted from 1946 until 1991, was between the Soviets and their allies and the West, mainly America and its allies.

Kleptomania

This is the urge to steal items of not very great value. Some kleptomaniacs are not even aware that they have committed a theft. Poirot uses this term very early on in the novel to explain the behaviour of a mysterious person who has taken strange objects from the hostel.

Student life

Students mostly leave home to go to university. Accommodation is varied at universities. Depending on the type of university, you can either live on campus, live in college, or more commonly share a house with other students. Students each rent a room in a house and share bills. In this novel, the students rent a hostel which is a cheaper form of accommodation.

Baker Street

Baker Street is a famous street in London. It is in the Marylebone area of the City of Westminster. The fictional detective Sherlock Holmes lived at a fictional 221B Baker Street address. The lost property office, where items left on the London transport system are collected, is located at Baker Street Station. More than 184,000 items are handed in to the lost property office every year!

Cinderella

Cinderella or *The Glass Slipper* is a well-known children's fairytale. Cinderella lives with her evil stepsisters in poverty and is not allowed to go to the ball. However, a fairy godmother appears and, wearing a beautiful dress, Cinderella does eventually go to the ball, where she meets the prince. But she must leave the ball at midnight, because her clothes will become rags again. Cinderella loses a shoe as she leaves. In the novel Colin points out that Cinderella loses a shoe when leaving the ball. Sally's shoe goes missing when she prepares for a party. Cinderella's shoe is returned to her when the Prince realizes that the shoe fits her perfectly.

Inquest

In cases of sudden, violent or suspicious death, it is common to hold a public inquiry called an inquest to find out why the person died. The coroner is the person in charge of the inquest, and the official cause of death is decided by a jury of twelve ordinary people chosen from the local community.

At the inquest the coroner and the jury hear medical evidence, as well as evidence from any other people that may be relevant. The family of the person who died, and members of the public, can also attend the inquest.

Once all the evidence has been heard, the jury gives its verdict – for example: natural death (e.g. a heart attack), accidental death, suicide, or murder.

Coutts

Coutts & Co. (commonly abbreviated to Coutts) is one of the UK's private banking houses, now owned by the Royal Bank of Scotland (RBS).

Dangerous drugs

Hyoscine is a drug which has been used for the treatment of abdominal pain.

Digitalis is a drug which has been used for the treatment of heart conditions.

Morphine is a drug to relieve pain. It is highly addictive.

Dangerous and poisonous drugs are now controlled much more carefully than they were when the story was written, and are not used so often.

The structure of the police in England

The structure of the police force and the ranks of the men and women who work in it are almost exactly the same as when the Metropolitan Police was created for London in 1829. The ranks, starting at the lowest, are: Police Constable, Sergeant, Inspector, Chief Inspector, Superintendent, Chief Superintendent.

Hitch-hiking

It is common for people, especially students, to hitch-hike around Europe. This is a cheap form of transport as you don't have to pay the person who stops to give you a lift. There are, however, disadvantages. You may have to wait around, often for long periods of time, before a driver will stop, and if you are hitch-hiking alone it can be dangerous.

Hickory Dickory Dock

Hickory Dickory Dock is a popular nursery rhyme. These are the original words:

Hickory, dickory, dock,
The mouse ran up the clock.
The clock struck one,
The mouse ran down,
Hickory, dickory, dock.

Nigel plays with the words of the original nursery rhyme. He has clearly chosen the poem because they live on Hickory Road and he is wondering who committed the murder, and when they will eventually stand in the dock, in court. Nigel's version also rhymes: 'Hickory, dickory, dock, the mouse ran up the clock. The police said "Boo", I wonder who, will eventually stand in the dock?'

Bridegroom, bride, best man

Right at the end of the story we hear that Sally and Len will be getting married. Cinderella lost her shoe, but then the prince found her and they got married. In a similar way Sally lost her shoe, it was then found and now she is getting married. Len is the bridegroom and Sally is the bride. Sally and Len ask Akibombo to be the best man for their wedding. The best man is the person who gives the bridegroom and bride their rings.

Glossary

Key

n = noun

v = verb

phr v = phrasal verb

adj = adjective

adv = adverb

excl = exclamation

exp = expression

acid (n)

a chemical substance, usually a liquid, which contains hydrogen and can react with other substances to form salts; some acids can burn you

accusation (n)

if you make an accusation against someone, you express the belief that they have done something wrong

admirer (n)

a person who likes and respects you

alibi (n)

proof that you were somewhere else when a crime was committed and the reason why you can't be **guilty** of a crime

balcony (n)

a platform on the outside of a building with a wall or railing around it

bet (n)

an agreement made between people when one person says they can do something, but the other person thinks they cannot. In some cases, whoever is wrong must give the other person money.

bicarbonate of soda (n)

a white powder which can be used as a stomach medicine

boiler (n)
device which burns fuel to provide hot water

boracic powder (n)
a white powder that dissolves in water, which has medicinal uses

brandy (n)
a strong alcoholic drink

bridegroom (n)
a man who is getting married (see Cultural notes)

candle (n)
a stick of hard wax with a piece of string through the middle. You light the string so the candle produces light.

charm (n)
quality of being attractive and pleasant

cheat (v)
behave dishonestly

cheque book (n)
a book of cheques (printed forms on which you write an amount of money and to whom the money is to be paid)

clarity (n)
the quality of being clear and easy to understand

clue (n)
something that helps you find the answer to a puzzle or mystery

Communist (n)
a supporter of the political belief that all people are equal and that workers should control the means of producing things (see Cultural notes)

complex (n)
a mental or emotional problem

confession (n)
the act of admitting that you have done something that you are ashamed of or embarrassed about

congratulate (v)
to express pleasure for something good that has happened to someone, or to praise them for something they have achieved

Coutts Bank (n)
a bank for wealthy people (see Cultural notes)

creature (n)
an animal, but used here ironically to describe a beautiful person

criminology (n)
the scientific study of crime and criminals

cruise (n)
a holiday spent on a ship or boat

cure (n)
medicine or other treatment that relieves an illness

cure (v)
to make a person change their ways

dictate (v)
to say something aloud for someone else to write down

digitalis (n)
a dangerous drug (see Cultural notes)

divorce (n)
the legal ending of a marriage

disapprove of (v)
to not be happy about something or someone

dock (n)
the place where a person accused of a crime sits or stands in a court room

eliminate (v)
to remove

engagement (n)
an agreement that two people have made to get married

evidence (n)
information from documents, objects, or witnesses, which is used in a court of law to try to prove something

fairy godmother (n)
a fictional character from the fairy story *Cinderella*, who helps Cinderella with her problems by using magic (see Cultural notes)

false (adj)
something which is artificial, but which is intended to look like the real thing or to be used instead of the real thing

fingerprint (n)
a mark made by a person's finger which shows the lines on the skin and can be used to identify criminals

fond of (adj)
when you like a person or thing

forge (v)
to make **false** copies

fortune-teller (n)
someone who predicts a person's future

free love (n)
a social movement which rejects marriage

frown (v)
to move your eyebrows close together because you are annoyed, worried, or thinking hard

gambler (n)
someone who bets money on the result of a game, a race, or competition

gasp (v)
to take a short, quick breath through your mouth

guilty (adj)
having committed a crime

handkerchief (n)
a small square of material which you use for blowing your nose

heroin (n)
a powerful, addictive drug

hitch-hike (n)
a form of travel which involves getting lifts from passing vehicles without having to pay (see Cultural notes)

hostel (n)
a large house where people can stay cheaply for a short time

hyoscine (n)
a dangerous drug (see Cultural notes)

incriminate (v)
to show someone is responsible for a crime

inquest (n)
a meeting where **evidence** is heard about someone's death to find out why they died

justice (n)
the system by which people are judged in courts of law and criminals are punished

kleptomaniac (n)
a person who cannot control their desire to steal things

label (n)
a piece of paper or plastic that is attached to an object, giving information about it

larceny (n)
the crime of stealing

lavatory (n)
a toilet

lecture (n)
an educational talk

light bulb (n)
the glass part of an electric lamp which gives out light when electricity passes through it

lining (n)
material attached to the inside of something

lipstick (n)
coloured make-up which women put on their lips

mood (n)
the way you feel

morphia (n)
an old-fashioned word for morphine, a very strong drug used for stopping pain (see Cultural notes)

motive (n)
the reason for doing something

moustache (n)
the hair that grows on a man's upper lip

nod (v)
to move your head up and down to show you understand or agree

nonsense (n)
something that is untrue or silly

odd (adj)
strange

offend (v)
to upset or embarrass someone

offending (adj)
upsetting or embarrassing

pharmacist (n)
a person who is qualified to prepare and sell medicines

pharmacy (n)
a place where medicines are sold or given out

physiotherapist (n)
a person whose job is to treat people with problems with their bones and muscles

powder compact (n)
a container for the make-up powder that a woman puts on her face

prescription (n)
a form on which the doctor writes the details of a medicine that has to be taken

prevention (n)
the act of making sure that something doesn't happen

principle (n)
a belief

profit (n)
an amount of money that you gain when you are paid more for something than it cost you

property (n)
things that belong to people

protest (n)
the act of saying or showing publicly that you do not approve of something

pulse (n)
the regular beating of the heart as it pumps blood through your body, which can be felt, for example, at the wrist or neck

quarrel (v)
to have an angry argument

rags (n)
old torn clothes

religious (adj)
a religious person has a strong belief in a god or gods

rucksack (n)
a bag used for carrying things on your back

safe (n)
a strong metal cupboard with special locks, in which money, jewellery, or other valuable things are kept

scholarship (n)
where studies are paid for by the school or university, or by some other organization

seam (n)
a line of stitches joining two pieces of cloth together

search warrant (n)
a legal document which allows the police to search a place

shellfish (n)
small creatures that live in the sea that can be eaten

silk (adj)
made of a very smooth, fine cloth made from a substance produced by a kind of moth

smuggling (n)
taking things into or out of a place illegally or secretly

sofa (n)
a comfortable seat with a back and arms, which two or three people can sit on

spy (n)
a person whose job is to find out secret information about another country or organization

stethoscope (n)
an instrument a doctor uses to listen to the heart and to breathing

suicide (n)
people who commit suicide deliberately kill themselves because they do not want to continue living

suspect (v)
to believe something unpleasant about someone

temper (n)
ability to become angry easily

tool (n)
a piece of equipment

unforgiving (adj)
unwilling to forgive or pardon others

victim (n)
someone who has been hurt or killed, usually as a result of a crime

zircon (n)
a mineral that looks like a diamond but is much less expensive

COLLINS ENGLISH READERS

The Agatha Christie Series

The Mysterious Affair at Styles
The Man in the Brown Suit
The Murder of Roger Ackroyd
The Murder at the Vicarage
Peril at End House
Why Didn't They Ask Evans?
Death in the Clouds
Appointment with Death
N or M?
The Moving Finger
Sparkling Cyanide
Crooked House
They Came to Baghdad
They Do It With Mirrors
A Pocket Full of Rye
After the Funeral
Destination Unknown
Hickory Dickory Dock
4.50 From Paddington
Cat Among the Pigeons